RAMOSE

AND THE TOMB ROBBERS

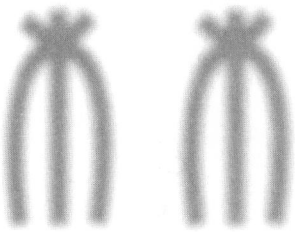

CAROLE WILKINSON

About the Author

Carole Wilkinson is an award-winning writer of over thirty books and TV scripts. She is interested in the history of everything and finds the hardest thing about writing books is to stop doing the research. She collects teapots and lives in Melbourne, Australia, with her husband, daughter and a spotty dog called Mitzie.

For John and Lili

RAMOSE

AND THE TOMB ROBBERS

CAROLE WILKINSON

CATNIP BOOKS
Published by Catnip Publishing Ltd.
Islington Business Centre
3-5 Islington High Street
London N1 9LQ

This edition published 2006
1 3 5 7 9 10 8 6 4 2

First published in Australia in 2001 by black dog books,
71 Gertrude Street, Fitzroy Vic 3065

A CIP catalogue record for this book is available from the
British Library

ISBN 10: 1 84647 001 3
ISBN 13: 978 1 84647 001 1

Printed in Poland

CONTENTS

1	IBIS EGGS AND HONEY CAKES	1
2	FURY OF THE GODS	13
3	AFTERMATH	24
4	RIVER JOURNEY	37
5	AN ANCIENT SCROLL	46
6	KIDNAPPED	55
7	THE SECRETS OF THE PYRAMID	64
8	THE DEAD PHARAOH	76
9	THE TOMB OF THE PRINCESS	86
10	UNDERGROUND	102
11	RETURN TO THE RIVER	116
	A WORD FROM THE AUTHOR	130
	GLOSSARY	131

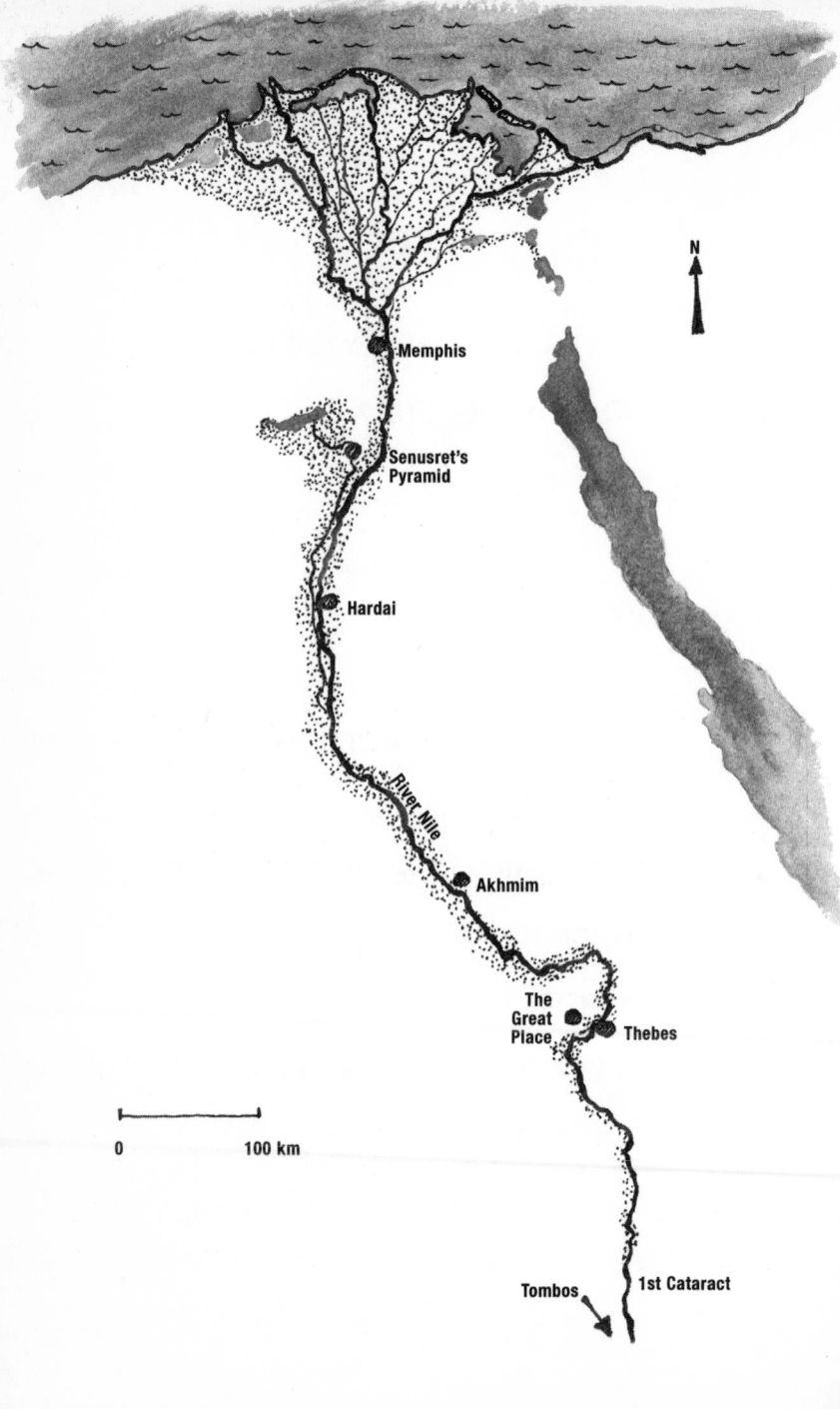

IBIS EGGS AND HONEY CAKES

"I WANT a cat," said Karoya.

"What for?" Ramose was sitting in the garden eating breakfast.

The small square of sunbaked sand at the back of Scribe Paneb's house, where Ramose and Karoya lived, hardly deserved to be called a garden. It was really an outdoor kitchen. The only things growing there were a struggling row of onions and a few herbs. The rest of the garden was just dry trodden earth. In one corner was the conical oven where Karoya baked bread for the household and the curved stone on which she ground grain every day. That's what Karoya was doing as Ramose watched her. She was on her hands and knees rolling a smooth round stone over the wheat grains that were sprinkled on the curved grinding stone. It was hard work. Karoya sat up on her heels to rest for a moment. She wiped her sweating brow on a fold of the red and green striped length of cloth that she wore draped over her head and massaged her back with her fingertips. Ramose would have liked to help her with her work, but Karoya was a slave. It wouldn't have been right for him to do a slave's work.

"A cat would eat the mice," replied Karoya. "Stop them from ruining the grain."

"You just want a pet," smiled Ramose.

"I do not! It would scare away snakes."

"We've managed without a cat before," said Ramose. "Why do you suddenly need one?"

Karoya went back to her grinding. After a while she spoke again. "It would be nice to have something that is just mine."

It was the first time Ramose had ever heard Karoya wish for anything. She was the property of Pharaoh, taken from her homeland of Kush and brought to Egypt to work as a slave. She owned nothing but the clothes she wore.

"I suppose Prince Ramose had dozens of cats back at the palace," said Karoya sulkily.

Ramose looked around anxiously. "Sssh. Don't ever call me that. Someone might hear."

"Well did you?"

"There were several cats, yes. But I had a pet monkey."

Karoya didn't look impressed.

"Where I come from there are lots of monkeys. They are a nuisance. They eat the dates and steal food. People chase them away. There are no cats though."

Ramose's monkey had come from Kush as well. Like Karoya, the monkey had been taken from the land of Kush because it suited Pharaoh. The life Ramose had lived as a prince seemed so long ago it was like another lifetime. Actually it wasn't long ago at all. Only eight months earlier his home had been the palace in the city. For all of his eleven years he had lived the pampered life of Pharaoh's son, heir to the throne of Egypt. He had been a different person then, spoilt and thoughtless, taking everything for granted. He'd had no worries—and he certainly hadn't had a slave for a friend. Things had changed since then.

Ramose's tutor, Keneben, and Heria, his beloved nanny, had been sure that Queen Mutnofret was trying to kill him. She was one of Pharaoh's lesser wives and she wanted her own son to be the next pharaoh. Ramose's two older brothers had already died. Keneben and Heria believed that Mutnofret had killed the older princes. They had begun testing Ramose's food on his pet monkey. Ramose knew nothing about this until the day he'd found his monkey dead.

Keneben and Heria had faked Ramose's death and sent him into hiding for safety. He was now living in secret as an apprentice scribe in the Great Place, the desert valley that his father had chosen as the place for his own tomb and the tombs of all future pharaohs.

At first he'd been comforted to know that he had friends at the palace. Then his nanny had died and Queen Mutnofret had sent Keneben to a foreign land. Ramose was on his own now. Only his sister, Hatshepsut, knew he was still alive and that one day he intended to be pharaoh.

His past and his future both seemed very distant. At the moment Ramose had to deal with his present life. He worked eight-day shifts at the tomb site along with the sculptors, painters and quarry men who were constructing his father's tomb. He had just finished his two-day break and was about to return to the tomb for another shift.

"I better get going," said Ramose finishing the last of his figs.

"I'll see you when I come up to the Great Place," said Karoya. She had to grind grain and do other work at the tomb site.

Ramose walked through the house. The scribe was still eating his breakfast.

"I'll go on ahead, Paneb," Ramose said.

The scribe said something with his mouth full of bread. Ramose didn't understand it, but he nodded anyway. He walked out of the village. His friend Hapu was waiting for him.

"Where's the scribe?" asked Hapu.

"He's still stuffing his face," said Ramose scornfully. "He's too fat and slow. Let him come at his own speed."

The two boys set off together on the dusty path to the Great Place.

Hapu was an apprentice painter at Pharaoh's tomb. He'd only found out a few weeks before that his friend was actually a prince—he was still getting used to the idea.

The construction of Pharaoh's tomb had been going on for three years. The quarry men had painstakingly chiselled out a long sloping shaft that cut deep into the rock of the valley. At the end of the shaft was a burial chamber and storage rooms where the goods for Pharaoh's afterlife would be stored. Everything Pharaoh needed would be packed into those rooms. There would be furniture, chariots, fine clothing and games. And of course rich and beautiful crowns, collars and armbands, so that he could live in the afterlife as he had in the world. The tomb was nearly finished.

When they reached the tomb, Hapu immediately disappeared into its depths to start work. He was painting the borders of the scenes painted on the tomb walls—which was all an apprentice was permitted to do. Ramose walked over to the store room where he collected an oil lamp and a fresh ink block. Outside the tomb entrance was a pile of stone flakes that the quarry men had chipped from the inside of the tomb. Ramose used the stone flakes to write on, as papyrus was too expensive for these daily tasks. The pile of stone flakes was just one of several piles and was higher than his head. He would never run out of writing materials. Only Paneb's monthly reports to the vizier were written on papyrus. Ramose selected a thin piece of stone about the size of his hand. He would use it for his first task of the day, making a list of all the men who had reported for work.

He lit his lamp, took a deep breath and started to walk down the dark shaft. Ramose didn't like being underground. He felt okay in the shaft, where he could see the square of light which was the tomb entrance. When he had to go into the burial chamber, though, he always felt a wave of panic and imagined that the tons of rock above his head were about to fall in on top of him, burying him alive. He turned round to look back at the tomb entrance. He was all right.

There were other lamps at intervals down the shaft and, about halfway down, there was a larger pool of light. A team of sculptors was carving the walls of the shaft. They were carefully chipping away the soft rock with copper chisels, following the rough drawings sketched on the surface by outliners.

Ramose stopped to write a list of the sculptors' names on his stone flake. He took a reed pen from his pen box. He chewed on the end to make sure that it had a nice soft brush and dipped it in the small container of water that he carried. Then he rubbed the pen onto the new block of black ink which he'd set into his palette. He wrote down the sculptors' names in his untidy handwriting.

"Be careful down there, Ramose," said one of the sculptors. "You never know when the ceiling might collapse and bring the whole mountain down on your head."

The sculptors all laughed. They thought it was very amusing that a tomb worker was afraid of enclosed spaces. Ramose was used to their jokes. He continued on down the tomb shaft.

Next was a group of painters who were bringing the sculptures to life with their bright colours. Ramose noted down their names as well.

At the bottom of the shaft was a chamber with the ceiling covered in yellow stars. Painters were working on the walls, painting prayers asking the gods to help Pharaoh journey safely through the underworld. Ramose turned to look back up the shaft. The square of light that was the tomb entrance looked small enough to fit in his hand. He took another deep breath and turned away from the light and descended the steps to the burial chamber. As quickly as he could, he noted down the tomb workers who were working in there, including Hapu, and then hurried out, back to where he could see the square of daylight again.

Ramose spent the morning checking all the painted texts to make sure that the painters had copied them correctly.

"I think I'll have my meal here in the tomb today," said Paneb at midday.

Paneb avoided walking up and down the tomb shaft as much as possible.

"Bring me down some food, Ramose."

Ramose didn't argue. When he'd first come to work in the tomb the muscles in his legs had been painfully sore. Now he'd walked up and down the steep slope of the tomb shaft so many times that he hardly noticed it. The muscles in his legs had grown strong.

"What's the special occasion?" Ramose asked the cook when he returned from delivering the scribe's food and could finally attend to his own meal. He looked hungrily at the unusually lavish spread of food.

"It's the feast day of Bastet, the cat goddess," said the cook, who used to be a sculptor until he'd lost two fingers when part of a tomb had collapsed. "No one celebrates it down here in the south, but in the Delta where I come from there's a big festival. I like to make something special for the goddess on her day."

Ramose helped himself to the food that was spread out for the workers' midday meal. He heaped freshly cooked lamb, bean stew and boiled eggs into his bowl.

"Pity it's not Bastet's feast day every day," he said. He felt something soft and warm brushing around his legs. A sleek, sandy-coloured creature with eyes the colour of greenstone was wrapping itself around Ramose's legs. It was the cook's cat. It had a gold earring in one delicately pointed ear. On a leather string around its neck was a small ceramic square with a Horus eye painted on it. This was to protect the animal from danger. The cat was miaowing loudly.

"Mery likes lamb," said the cook, smiling at his pampered pet. "She wouldn't mind if you shared a bit with her."

"I like lamb too," said Ramose, thinking that the cook's cat looked well-fed enough.

Hapu was piling a second helping into his own bowl. He couldn't help staring at the way the cook managed to do things with his three-fingered hand.

"What are these?" Ramose asked pointing to a pile of sticky balls on a platter, hoping the man hadn't seen Hapu staring.

"They're fig and nut cakes," the cook replied. "Rolled in honey. And there won't be enough for all the workers if your friend takes so many."

Hapu put two of the sticky balls back on the platter and licked his fingers. He and Ramose walked back to their hut and sat down to eat. The hut was nothing more than a pile of rocks roofed over with a few palm fronds, but it was the boys' home while they were in the Great Place. Ramose picked up one of the large eggs.

"I haven't eaten an ibis egg since I was at—"

Hapu dug him in the ribs. "Samut's over there," he whispered. "Watch what you're saying."

Ramose glanced over his shoulder. The foreman of the tomb was talking to another tomb worker. Ramose was normally more careful. He peeled his egg and bit into it.

"Save one of your cakes for Karoya," Ramose said. "I'd like to take some home for her."

Hapu looked at his friend. "Why should I give my food to her?"

"She probably hasn't tasted anything like them," said Ramose.

The cat came and sat next to Ramose watching very closely as he ate his food. It miaowed again. It wasn't a polite request, it was a demand. Ramose gave it a piece of meat to keep it quiet. The cat ate it delicately.

"Karoya would like a cat like this," he said.

"I've never met anyone so concerned about a slave," grumbled Hapu pushing one of the sweet cakes to the side of his bowl.

"I feel responsible for her. If my father's army hadn't captured her, she'd still be living in freedom with her family in Kush."

"Pharaoh's army has captured thousands of slaves. What difference does it make if one of them is a little happier than the rest?"

"It makes a difference to me," replied Ramose, then he lowered his voice. "When I become pharaoh, the first thing I will do is free her."

"What about the other thousands of slaves?" asked Hapu eating his last fig cake.

Ramose thought for a moment. It would be hard being pharaoh, there would be so many difficult decisions to make.

"I'll free them all," he replied.

"And who will grind the grain?" asked Hapu.

"I'll let the vizier worry about that."

2

FURY OF
THE GODS

HAPU FINISHED his food and put his bowl
down in the sand. He sighed contentedly
and leaned back against the wall of the
hut with his hands behind his head. His smile
faded slightly.

"The sky's a strange colour."

Ramose looked up at the large oval of sky above
the valley. It was darkening. Light grey clouds

were drifting over the valley. A breeze suddenly picked up. It was more than a breeze. It was a wind strong enough to blow over one of the water jars. It wasn't the hot wind that occasionally blew from the desert. It was cool. Ramose shivered.

"What's happening?" asked Hapu.

There was a low rumble in the distance. The clouds grew darker as they moved across the valley and covered the sun. As they stared at the sky the boys saw a flash of bright light zigzag from the clouds to the pyramid-shaped peak of the mountain known as the Gate of Heaven. The rumbling noise came again and grew until it exploded in a loud crack.

"The gods must be angry," said Hapu. He was plainly terrified. "They're attacking us."

The sky above the valley was completely covered with black clouds. It was like evening instead of midday. More lightning flashed around the mountain followed immediately by a louder crack of thunder. A large drop of water fell on Ramose's upturned face. Then another. Within a few seconds water was pouring from the sky.

"It's raining," Ramose said, hardly able to believe his eyes.

Hapu stared in amazement as the large drops of water falling from the sky were replaced by even larger lumps of ice. Round ice stones the size of walnuts started pelting down on them.

"Quick," yelled Ramose. "The tomb. We can shelter in the tomb."

The boys ran towards the tomb entrance. Other tomb workers were doing the same. The cook, abandoning his cooking pots, picked up the cat and ran with the boys. They reached the tomb and watched in disbelief as the ice stones continued to fall. The tomb workers shook their heads. The cook's cat was yowling loudly, adding to the eerie feeling that something terrible was about to happen.

"This is a bad omen," said one of the sculptors. "I've heard of rain falling in the desert before, but I've never heard of anything like this."

Ramose remembered when he was younger seeing a heavy shower of rain on a royal visit to the northern city of Memphis. Hapu, who had lived all his life in the south, had never seen rain before. In Egypt people were used to their water coming from the Nile, not from the sky. If the gods were throwing ice stones at them, it was indeed a bad sign.

The ice stones stopped as suddenly as they started and were replaced by rain again, even heavier than before.

"The earth will be covered with water. We'll drown," said Hapu who was almost in tears.

"It'll stop soon," said Ramose, trying to reassure his friend, but he was scared himself.

As if to contradict Ramose's words, there was another rumbling noise. This time it didn't come from the sky but from the ground. It didn't fade or end in a crack, it grew. It was coming from the direction of the Gate of Heaven, the cobra goddess's mountain home.

Ramose watched the familiar slopes of the mountain turn to liquid mud as water foamed down them. Then a wave of water appeared over the edge of the high desert on the western side of the mountain and rushed down its slopes in a foamy surge. The ground beneath their feet began to shake. The noise of the advancing water turned from a rumble to a roar as water continued to pour from the high desert down the mountain slopes. As the size of the wave grew, so did the noise.

It was like nothing Ramose had ever heard before, deafening and frightening. A wall of water crashed down the lower slopes and began to surge across the valley floor. The water was brown with mud. Stones and rocks were carried along in the flow, gouging a deep rut in the sand. Boulders the size of houses were washed down from the slopes of the mountain as if they were pebbles. The wall of water was rushing across the valley at such a speed that Ramose and the other tomb workers stood and stared at it in disbelief.

As it got closer the wave grew bigger. Ramose

calculated that it must be at least ten cubits high. The cook's cat yowled again and struggled out of her master's arms and darted out of the tomb. Ramose suddenly realised that the terrible wave was heading straight for them.

"We have to get to higher ground," Ramose yelled, "or we'll be washed away."

The tomb makers suddenly leapt to life and ran out of the tomb entrance. They didn't have time to get across the valley to the path that led to the village. Instead they followed the cat which was clambering up the cliffs around the tomb entrance. Hapu didn't move, he was mesmerised by the awful brown wave.

"Hapu, come on!" shouted Ramose, but the roar of the approaching water drowned his feeble voice.

Ramose grabbed his friend's arm and pulled him along. Hapu finally tore his eyes away from the water and started scrambling up the cliff. The rain battered down on them. Rivulets of water pouring down the cliff loosened stones, making it hard for them to climb. Every time they grabbed a stone for a handhold it would slip out of its muddy hole and fall to the valley floor.

Ramose turned to look for Hapu who was struggling below him. The wall of brown water was coursing across the valley. The storehouse and the workers' makeshift huts were smashed by the crest of the wave. The place where minutes before they had sat in the sun eating their meal disappeared beneath the surging water.

The wave would be on them in a few seconds. Ramose looked for a way up the sheer cliff face. Water was sluicing down it like a waterfall. Other men were trying to climb up the cliff, but it was too steep and slippery with rain. He saw someone slip and fall. He knew that if he didn't think of something quickly he and his friend would face the same fate.

The familiar dirty-yellow colour of the cliff had turned brown in the rain. Ramose saw a darker brown stripe in the rock face to his left. It was a crevice, a vertical split in the cliff. Hapu's hands were groping wildly around Ramose's feet. Ramose reached down, grabbed his friend's arm and yanked him up. He shouted at him, telling him to shelter in the crevice. His words were completely swallowed by the roar of the water. Hapu was blinking the rain out of his eyes, too frightened and stunned to comprehend what Ramose was trying to do.

Ramose pushed Hapu into the crevice, but didn't have time to squeeze in himself. The wave of water hit the cliff with a crushing force. Ramose glimpsed other workers washed from the cliff as the side of his head crashed against the rock. Gritty water filled his mouth and nose. He couldn't move. The weight of the water pushed him against the rock. I'm going to die, he thought, squashed like an insect under god's thumb.

The wave split into two streams around the cliff face and Ramose felt himself being ripped off the cliff face by one of the streams and washed along in its furious course. The tumbling water tossed him like a reed. There was water all around him. He couldn't tell which way the surface was. He tried to scream out in terror, but only got a mouthful of muddy water.

Ramose felt the grasping hands of drowning men grab at his arms and legs. Now he knew which way was down. I don't want to die, he thought. He kicked out to stop them dragging him down with them. His lungs were ready to burst. He opened his eyes. He could see nothing but murky brown water. He kicked again and his head broke the surface.

He gulped in air, but still couldn't see through the sand and silt that filled his eyes. He reached out blindly. His hand banged against stone as the stream dragged him along and his fingers struck a protruding rock. He grabbed at it with both hands and heaved himself up onto it. The rushing water pulled at him, but he clung to the rock gasping for air. He felt sharp points stick into his back and then something climbing up his back and onto his shoulder.

By the time Ramose had blinked the sand out of his eyes the rain had stopped. The water still rushed past, but it was losing its force. There was a forlorn yowling in his ear. He reached up to his shoulder. There was something clinging there, covered with wet fur. It was the cook's cat, terrified but still alive. Ramose straddled the rock with the wet cat in his arms. A feeling of elation burst inside him, he wanted to shout out loud. He was alive, he'd cheated death. The gods had poured down their fury and he had survived.

The water was disappearing, oozing through cracks and ravines, soaking into the sand. The sky was a strange orange colour as the sun fought to break through the thinning clouds. It cast an unearthly light on the Great Place. The rocks shone. The valley was an unfamiliar place. The rushing waters had completely resculpted the valley floor with wet sand and huge boulders. The remains of the huts and the storehouse were buried under two cubits of brown mud. A deep ravine had been cut down the middle of the valley where the main force of the flood had bored along.

Ramose realised that he was naked. The flood waters had ripped his kilt from him. He could taste the metallic taste of blood in the water that dripped from his hair. Blood was seeping from cuts and grazes all over his body. He stood up shakily and looked around. Others emerged from

the shelter of the rocks. Ramose clambered stiffly
down the rock, dizzy with the joy of being alive.
He waded through the knee-deep sludge that was
now the new valley floor, still holding on to the
cat.

The mud sucked at Ramose's legs as he made
his way towards the tomb entrance. He couldn't
find it. It wasn't there any more. The cliff above it
had collapsed and fallen into the mud.

The mud around him grew too deep to wade
through. There was a soft moist noise like a
contented belch after a good meal. The bog
around him shifted slightly and a body floated
to the surface. The face was bruised and
battered beyond recognition, but one hand had
two fingers missing. Ramose's joy, turned to
horror and then to fear. He was alive, but others
had died. What about Hapu? He prayed to Amun,
king of the gods, that his friend was still alive.

The clouds moved away to the south and the
sun appeared again. The surviving tomb makers
slowly made their way to higher ground and
gathered together in a dazed and bruised group.
Ramose looked frantically at their faces. Hapu
wasn't among them. He clambered back down to
where he had left his friend. That section of the
cliff was still standing. Hapu was still wedged
in the crevice where Ramose had pushed him.
He gently pulled his friend out. His face was

covered in deep gashes, his nose was pushed to one side, his lip was split and pouring blood. His eyelids flickered as Ramose pulled him out into the sunlight. He was still alive, but unconscious. Ramose's face which had just dried in the sun, was wet again. This time with tears of relief. With the cat clinging to his shoulder, Ramose carried Hapu back to where the stunned survivors were huddled together.

A group of women and children from the village appeared on the rim of the valley. They had heard the terrible roar of the water from the village. Ianna, the scribe's wife, was among them, so was Karoya.

"Are you all right?" she said taking the striped cloth that she wore over her head and giving it to Ramose with her head turned away.

Ramose had forgotten that he was naked. He quickly wrapped the cloth around himself.

"Yes, I'm okay, but I'm not sure about Hapu." Ramose gently wiped the mud and blood from his friend's face.

Ianna was looking frantically from face to face.

"Where is Paneb?" she asked in a quavery voice.

Ramose hadn't given the scribe a thought. He had been down in the tomb when the storm hit. The scribe was fat and slow. He would have heard the roar of the approaching water, but would never have made it up the shaft in time. Ianna let out a wail that echoed around the valley. Other women who had been unable to find their husbands and fathers joined in. The eerie wailing gave Ramose goose skin, despite the fact that the sun had already dried and warmed him.

"What's that?" asked Karoya pointing to the damp, furry bulge in the crook of Ramose's arm.

"It's for you," he said and held out the cat to her.

3

AFTERMATH

THE STORM had lasted for only half an hour, but it had changed the lives of the tomb workers forever. Of the eighteen men who worked in Pharaoh's tomb, only six had survived the flood. Ten women had lost their husbands. Twenty-three children were fatherless. Hapu, whose mother had died the previous year, was orphaned. Pharaoh's tomb was ruined.

The heavy rain had damaged the village, mud bricks had melted away in the downpour, cellars had been flooded, but the damage was soon repaired. Hapu, though stunned, cut and bruised, was soon recovering.

Ianna wandered from room to room in the house, not knowing what to do with herself. "His soul will be lost," she cried. "He will never find peace."

Ramose hadn't liked the scribe much, but he would never have wished this on him. His body was buried under the great weight of stones and sand that the flood had washed into Pharaoh's tomb. There would be no mummy to place in the hillside tomb that Paneb had been preparing, at great expense, for his own burial.

"The sculptors will make a statue of Paneb to place in his tomb." Ramose had tried to console her. "His spirit will live in the statue. He will find peace."

Five days after the flood, Vizier Wersu stood in the valley of the Great Place on a pile of sand and rocks. The royal architect, a man called Ineni, was explaining the situation to him.

"The tomb entrance under us is buried beneath several cubits of sand and rocks. The sculptured walls will be cracked, scored and broken. The tomb itself will certainly be full of water. The burial chamber may have collapsed."

Ramose was standing at a respectful distance with the other surviving tomb workers trying to catch the architect's words.

"While the rocks and sand could eventually be removed," Ineni told them, "it would take years, decades, perhaps even a century, for the water to seep away."

The vizier said nothing. His thin mouth was grim. His bony insect hands were clasped behind his back.

"It is my recommendation, Vizier," continued the architect, "that a new tomb should be excavated with the entrance on higher ground." He said it as casually as if he was talking about weaving a new basket or making a stool.

There was a murmur among the tomb workers. They had all been working on Pharaoh's tomb for three years.

The vizier turned to the workers. Ramose kept to the back of the group. His face was cut and bruised and he didn't think the vizier would recognise him, but he didn't want to take the risk. Ramose avoided Wersu's evil eyes.

"I agree with Architect Ineni," said the vizier. "A new tomb must be commenced." He looked around at the battered and bruised team of workers as if he was bored with the situation. "There is another matter which is of importance to this project." He paused while he adjusted the folds of his robes.

"Pharaoh has fallen ill in Memphis. He is very ill. It is feared that he may be rested from life before the year's end."

Ramose stared at the vizier's dispassionate face. He might have been telling them that there was no beer for their midday meal or that the cost of chisels had increased.

For Ramose the news was staggering. His father was dying. When he died, Ramose would be the rightful heir to the kingship, but since everyone thought he was dead the crown would go to his half-brother, the horrible brat Tuthmosis.

"So then, work must start on the new tomb immediately," said the vizier.

The tomb workers turned to go back to the village. They knew they had a huge task in front of them, but they were Pharaoh's tomb builders and they were willing to do whatever they had to in order to finish his tomb in time.

"There is one more thing." The vizier's voice was thick with what sounded like pleasure.

The workers turned back.

"Pharaoh's new tomb is to be built with the entrance higher in the cliff face. It will be a difficult excavation. Time is short. You are now few."

He looked around at the six remaining tomb workers and the two apprentices. "I will send for the gangs of temple craftsmen working in Thebes and in Memphis. They will take charge of the work. You will be sent to work somewhere else."

The tomb workers stood in stunned silence for a moment as Vizier Wersu walked away and climbed into a covered chair. Four porters lifted the chair and carried the vizier away towards the city. The tomb workers all started shouting at once.

"They can't send us away."

"We are Pharaoh's tomb makers."

"This is our home!"

"Where will we be sent?" Ramose asked the architect.

"You have been appointed to Tombos," replied the architect. There was a shiver of exclamations through the small group. "You will have the honour of working on a fortress and temple commemorating Pharaoh's great victories over Egypt's enemies."

Ramose walked back to the tomb makers' village on legs that felt like they were made out of soft mud. He kept his distance from the other workers. He needed time to get used to these new circumstances. Only a week ago he'd thought of his life in the village as a tedious chore. He thought he would have done anything to get out of it. Now that it was suddenly all about to change, he found himself wishing it wasn't over.

He went back to the scribe's house. Ianna

was lying on a couch, weeping. Hapu came in and slowly lowered himself onto a stool. He was still weak and hadn't been to the meeting with Wersu.

"I've just walked around the garden," he said sounding exhausted.

Now that he had no family of his own, Hapu had been recovering in the scribe's house where Karoya could look after him. His injuries were worse than Ramose's. His face was still swollen and bruised, his broken nose permanently squashed sideways. His whole body was stiff and sore. Karoya came in with wine for her grieving mistress, beer for Ramose and a thick brown potion for her patient. The cat, Mery, followed closely at her heels.

Hapu pulled a face as he sipped at the potion. "I'm sure you're trying to poison me," he said to Karoya.

"It is a remedy from Kush, made from burnt lotus leaves and the fruit of the castor oil plant. It will help heal your body."

Hapu drank it down in one gulp. "What did the vizier say?" he asked.

"A new tomb is to be built," replied Ramose quietly.

Hapu nodded. It was what they had expected.

"And excavation has to start immediately," continued Ramose blankly. He was still numb with shock. "Pharaoh is dying."

Hapu and Karoya both turned to Ramose. They knew what this meant to him.

"May Osiris protect him," muttered Hapu.

"That's not the only thing," said Ramose. "New gangs will build the tomb. We will be sent to Tombos."

Hapu looked at Ramose in disbelief. "Tombos? Where's Tombos?" he asked. "I've never heard of this place."

Ramose had heard of it. He knew all the details of his father's campaigns. it was a small town only recently conquered by Pharaoh's army.

"It's a town at the very southern edge of Egypt, beyond the third cataract."

Hapu was stunned. "I've never been south of the city. I've never been north of it either. I've spent my whole life in Thebes. I thought I'd grow old here."

Hapu knew that the Nile, in its journey from its source deep in foreign lands, was not the silent, slow-moving river that they were familiar with. It was a noisy, foaming stream that cascaded over a series of rocky outcrops. These were known as the cataracts. Until Pharaoh's recent conquest, the first cataract had marked the edge of Egypt.

"I don't want to live beyond the third cataract," said Hapu. "That's in the lands of the barbarian sand-dwellers."

Karoya looked annoyed. "Why do Egyptians

think everyone outside their land is a barbarian? I should like to go to this place. It will be closer to my home."

"He doesn't mean to offend you, Karoya," Ramose said. "No one likes to leave their homeland."

The tomb makers and their families left the village after the funerals. Only two of the missing bodies had been found. They had been sent to Thebes for mummification. All the other men had had statues made for their tombs. This meant that they didn't have to wait the usual seventy days until the mummification process was complete. Now that they were used to the idea, the villagers seemed anxious to leave. Their few possessions were piled on a sled which the men took it in turns to pull.

Ramose could easily carry his possessions. He had slightly less than he'd had when he arrived at the village. Since he lost his kilt in the flood, he didn't even have a change of clothing. He still had the gold, melted down into thick rings, that Keneben had given him. He had the scribal tools that he'd used in the schoolroom back at the palace, but which had been too rich and ornate for him to use in the village without attracting attention. He also had his heart scarab hidden at the bottom of his bag. This was the large beetle-shaped jewel that was to be buried with him when he died. Hapu had taken a stool and a chest that his father had made. Karoya, the slave girl, had more baggage than either of them. She had a large bag which contained her favourite cooking pot and the round stone that she used for grinding grain. She was also carrying a basket made of woven rushes under her arm. The basket had an open grille woven into the lid to let air in.

"You shouldn't have brought that, Karoya," grumbled Hapu, who was now recovered enough to walk to Thebes. "Slaves aren't supposed to have possessions. You should be helping me carry my things."

"Carry your own baggage," Karoya snapped.

Ramose smiled as he listened to his friends bicker. He knew Hapu would never get the better of Karoya. Through the lid of Karoya's rush basket, Hapu could see two glinting green eyes. She was carrying the cat that Ramose had saved from the flood.

"Mery is mine," said Karoya firmly. "She comes with me."

The ragged group straggled up the path that led from the tomb makers' village to the city. They reached the top of the hill and the blue strip of the Nile was suddenly visible in the distance with a band of green vegetation on either side. The temples and the city were on the other side of the river. On this side was the palace, its white-washed walls dazzling in the sun, its gold-tipped flagpoles glinting. Ramose turned to look back at the village. From that height its mud brick walls seemed to merge with the valley floor. It was a strange place for a prince to have spent six months of his life. He was glad to be leaving the miserable little village, but, on the other hand, he wasn't sorry he had experienced living there.

"Come on, Ramose," Hapu called out. "You're getting left behind."

In less than half an hour Ramose was back in the familiar fertile Nile Valley that he hadn't seen for eight months. The landscape changed suddenly from dry, dusty desert to green fields and orchards. Ramose breathed in deeply.

"Smell that," he said to his friends. "Isn't it wonderful?"

The air was laden with the fragrance of pomegranates and slightly fermenting grapes. Karoya wrinkled her nose. She was a desert-dweller and the fertile smells of the river valley were strange to her.

"It smells sort of greenish," she said. "And the air is heavy."

They passed by the palace walls. Ramose looked up at the fluttering pennants and the high windows. Karoya and Hapu exchanged a glance. Ramose pictured its luxurious interiors: the massive halls and columns; the comfortable bed with the thick linen mattress; his own room with the wall paintings of Amun, king of the gods, and of his father hunting in the Delta. He wondered if his sister, Hatshepsut, was in the palace. More than likely she had travelled up to Memphis to be with their father. There was nothing for him at the palace now. His nanny was dead, his tutor sent abroad. He would be a stranger in his own home.

They reached the edge of the river and the foreman herded them onto a ferry made of bundles of papyrus reeds lashed together. Karoya was very anxious about getting onto the boat.

"We're just going across the river," said Ramose, trying to encourage her. "It's quite safe."

"I don't like the river," she said flatly. "Too much water is bad."

After his experience in the flood, Ramose could not argue with her. He helped her aboard and found her somewhere to sit, away from the sides of the boat. Mery was miaowing plaintively from her basket. It sounded like she shared her mistress's dislike of the river.

Ramose was happy to be on the river. He trailed his hand in its cool blue waters and felt the fresh breeze on his face.

They spent the night on the roof of Ianna's brother's house in the noisy, sprawling city.

Ianna was going to stay in Thebes and live with her brother. Karoya was to stay and serve her. Ramose and Hapu would be apprenticed to new workers in Tombos. The two boys were to leave the following morning, sailing south with the rest of the workers from the Great Place.

Ramose woke before daybreak and got up. He picked up his bag and quietly crept across the roof to the stairs. He looked back to check that he hadn't disturbed his friends and tripped over something soft and furry. Ramose crashed to the floor and Mery screeched with pain. Karoya and Hapu sat upright at the same time.

"What's going on?" said Hapu sleepily.

Karoya was wide awake immediately. "Where do you think you're going?" she said.

The sky was starting to lighten to the east and she could make out Ramose sprawled on the floor. He was wearing his cloak and his bag was slung over his shoulder. Mery jumped onto Karoya's lap and looked at Ramose as reproachfully as her mistress.

"I think that cat tripped me up on purpose," said Ramose getting to his feet.

"Of course she did," said Karoya. "She knew that you shouldn't be sneaking off in the night by yourself."

Ramose looked at the pink glow in the sky. "It isn't the night."

"What are you doing up so early?" asked Hapu rubbing his eyes. "The boat to Tombos doesn't leave till mid-morning."

"I'm not going to Tombos," said Ramose. "I'm going to Memphis to see my father."

4

RIVER
JOURNEY

"**A**ND YOU weren't even going to say goodbye?" Karoya was sitting with her arms folded crossly.

"I thought it would be better if you were as surprised as everyone else. I didn't want you to get into trouble."

"I'm coming with you," said Hapu, scrambling to his feet.

"I have to hurry," said Ramose gathering up his things. "The boat to Memphis leaves soon."

"I suppose once you're pharaoh you won't be interested in having an apprentice painter for a friend."

"Certainly not a slave."

"That's not true. I was just concerned about your safety. It'll be dangerous when I get to Memphis. I have enemies there. My father is ill. It won't be easy to get to see him."

His friends sat in silence.

"I'll send for both of you when it's safe. I promise."

"If it's going to be so difficult, you'll need help," said Hapu rolling up his reed mat. "And anything's better than going to Tombos."

Ramose didn't have time to argue. He couldn't decide whether he was glad or not that his friends were coming with him. He appreciated the company, but three people wandering around Egypt were a lot more obvious than one. They had to work out a story.

It was easy enough to get on the boat to Memphis. The boatman was happy to carry them without asking questions once he had one of Ramose's gold rings in his hand.

It was a long way to Memphis. The winds blew from the north, any boat sailing south only had to put up a sail to be carried down the Nile.

Travelling north wasn't so easy and the wooden boat had a crew of oarsmen to push it against the prevailing wind. They were away before most people were awake.

The journey was going to take two weeks at least. Ramose would have plenty of time to think about what he would do when he arrived in the northern city. The boatman was very curious about his young passengers. Ramose told him the story that they had invented—that he and Hapu had been apprenticed to workers at the temple of Ptah. He pulled out a scroll of papyrus and showed the boatman. The boatman looked at the squiggly writing and the important-looking red seal on the bottom and nodded.

"The old temple is being rebuilt," said Ramose. Hapu nodded knowledgeably. "The slave girl will cook for us on our journey." Karoya tried to look like an obedient servant.

The boatman looked suspiciously at Mery, who was miaowing loudly and unhappily from her basket.

"A present for the lady of the household where we will be staying," explained Ramose. Hapu nodded again.

The boatman seemed satisfied with their story and went off to shout at the oarsmen.

Hapu waited until he was well out of earshot before he spoke. "That papyrus is the list of food sent to the Great Place from the city last month!"

Ramose grinned. "I knew he wouldn't be able to read."

"So I am your slave as usual," said Karoya.

"You *are* a slave, Karoya," said Hapu. "What else was he supposed to say?"

"He could have said I was a princess from Kush going to pay tribute to Pharaoh."

"I don't think you're quite dressed for the part. And where are all your servants, Your Highness?"

"Stop arguing, you two," said Ramose. "The boatman will hear."

He glanced over at the boatman who was now settling down for a rest.

"You will have to be our slave while we are travelling, Karoya. Anything else would just attract attention. I promise you that as soon as I am pharaoh, the first thing I will do is grant you freedom and see that you are returned to your homeland."

They were the only passengers on the boat. The boat had a cargo of logs, precious hardwood from the southern lands. After they had been travelling for two days, Karoya let Mery out of her basket. The cat sniffed around the boat suspiciously, but soon got used to the idea of living on a boat. Karoya was still uncomfortable with so much water around her. She sat in the middle of the boat with her eyes fixed firmly on the shore.

Ramose and Hapu fished and played senet. They watched the land slip by them on either side. They saw brief scenes from people's lives as they passed: women pounding dirty clothes with rocks, a man trying to move a stubborn ox, a child crying over a lost ball that was floating out of reach.

Each evening the boat was moored and Karoya went off in search of dry reeds and animal dung to make a cooking fire. They ate a simple meal of bread and fish, and then slept on the boat on their reed mats. When they stopped at a town they bought more food. Ramose had exchanged two of his gold rings for copper. It attracted too much attention when they offered gold in exchange for flour and vegetables.

The journey was taking longer than Ramose had expected. After a week on board the boat, they had only reached Akhmim, which by Ramose's reckoning was only a third of the way to Memphis. At this rate it was going to take a lot of gold to keep the three of them fed on the journey. Actually there were four mouths to feed as Mery had to have a daily supply of fish and milk.

"Look," whispered Hapu as if he had read Ramose's thoughts. "Over there."

Ramose looked over to where Hapu was pointing. A rat was walking calmly along the edge of the boat. It hopped from there onto one of the logs strapped to the deck. Mery was curled up asleep in her open basket totally unaware of the rat.

"Did you see that?" said Hapu to Karoya. "There was a rat. That cat of yours didn't even notice it! It's useless. All it does is eat our food, drink our milk and make that awful wailing noise when we're trying to sleep."

"Sounds a bit like you," said Karoya scratching Mery behind the ear.

"I don't wail," said Hapu.

Ramose ignored his friends' bickering and returned to his thoughts. He knew he'd need gold to bribe people once he got to the palace if he was going to get anywhere near his father. He wondered if his supply of gold was enough.

"I'm bored," said Hapu. "How much further is it?"

Ramose was beginning to wish that he'd managed to sneak away on his own. Hapu and Karoya were either complaining about being on a boat for so long or arguing with each other.

"Nobody asked you to come," said Ramose irritably. "But just remember that if you weren't on this boat, Hapu, you'd be on another one heading for alien lands beyond the reaches of Egypt. And you, Karoya, would be Ianna's slave."

His friends didn't say anything. Ramose had to admit he was sick of the boat as well. It wasn't like the royal barge that had taken him up and down the river when he was still a prince. Then he'd had a comfortable bed, servants to attend to his slightest need, and as much food as he wished to eat.

Later that evening they were sitting on board the boat eating their evening meal.

"Can't we get some meat?" Hapu grumbled. "I'm sick of fish." He was just about to put a piece of fish in his mouth when Mery strode up importantly and dropped something in his lap. Hapu looked down. It was a dead rat. He leapt to his feet with a yell.

"You said you wanted meat!" said Karoya.

It was the first time Ramose had laughed in quite a while.

Another six days brought them to a town called Hardai. The royal barge had never stopped there. Ramose didn't like the look of it. It was just a collection of mud brick houses and dusty streets.

The people didn't smile, they were not friendly. Karoya got into an argument with a woman who was trying to sell her some rotten grapes when she wanted figs. The three friends walked back towards the boat and for once they were pleased to be getting back on board. The boatman was sitting on the wharf waiting for them. He looked up and grinned as they approached.

"It's going to cost you another twenty deben of copper to go all the way to Memphis," he said while picking at a scab on his hand.

Ramose looked at him in disbelief. "What are you talking about? We already paid you for the whole trip."

"The winds have been stronger than expected," said the boatman. "It's taking longer than I thought."

"What difference does that make?" shouted Hapu angrily. "We aren't eating your food."

"The extra weight is slowing us down."

"That's nonsense," said Ramose. "We weigh nothing compared to your cargo."

He jerked his head towards the huge logs on board the boat.

"And Mery has caught three rats since we've been on your dirty boat," added Karoya.

"An extra twenty deben or you stay here," said the boatman.

Ramose was furious. "Okay we stay here."

The boatman called his bluff. "I'm casting off."

"Go then," said Ramose stubbornly. "We'll find another boat going to Memphis."

"Hardai's not the place to spend the night outdoors," said the man, unwinding the rope that tied up his boat.

"Ramose," whispered Hapu. "There might not be another boat for days."

Ramose was too angry to listen to reason.

The boatman threw the rope on board. He jumped aboard himself.

"This is your last chance," he said.

Ramose said nothing.

"Row!" shouted the boatman to his oarsmen.

The boat moved away from the quay leaving the three companions stranded in Hardai.

5

AN ANCIENT
SCROLL

"I DON'T THINK that was a good idea," said Hapu as he watched the boat shrink into the distance.

The only other boats at the quay were local fishing boats made of papyrus reeds.

"Now what are we going to do?" moaned Hapu.

"We'll have to spend the night here," replied Ramose. "You were both desperate to get off that boat. Now we are off it, and you are still complaining."

"There's nowhere I can make a fire," said Karoya. "The streets are crowded and there's no open land. We'll have to walk into the countryside."

"I don't like the idea of that," said Ramose, looking at the unfriendly people. "We'll have to see if someone will sell us a cooked meal and maybe let us sleep on their roof.

Everywhere they asked, people wanted many deben of copper to let the travellers share their meagre meal and sleep on their roof. They stood in the dirty main street of the town. They were all starting to wish they were back on board the cargo boat.

"You don't want to stay in this place," said a voice at Ramose's shoulder. It was a short man with a beard and eyes that looked in different directions. "It's full of thieves."

"We don't have much choice," Ramose said. "There are no other boats leaving for the north."

"I'm aboard a naval boat, taking men up to the Delta," the man replied. "I could talk to the captain for you. I'm sure he wouldn't mind if you sailed with us. We've just stopped to buy some fresh meat. We'll be leaving again in about an hour."

The three friends returned to the wharf. While

they had been searching the town for somewhere to spend the night, the naval boat had tied up. It was a sleek craft. Ramose grinned at Hapu and Karoya as they boarded the boat. They couldn't believe their luck.

"This is more like it," said Hapu as they moved off.

The naval boat was bigger, cleaner and faster. It cut through the water at twice the speed of the cargo boat under the power of twenty soldiers at the oars. The captain stood at the stern shouting orders and operating the rudder oar.

They travelled until it was dark and then camped on the riverbank. Their camping place was away from any town or village and it was very peaceful. The soldiers invited them to share their food. After they'd eaten all the lamb and onions they could, they laid out their reed mats on the sandy shore beneath a grove of date palms.

"It's good to be away from that awful town," said Karoya looking up at the stars through the palm fronds.

"Maybe our luck's changed," said Hapu.

Ramose listened to the stillness of the night and hoped he was right.

Their new friend was called Hori. He was travelling with two other men. One was a big man called Intef, who seemed to have an excess of muscles, but a shortage of brains. The other was called Seth. He had a mean mouth and a scar on his neck as if someone had unsuccessfully tried to chop off his head.

"We're going to Memphis to join the navy," Hori told them over breakfast. "The captain is my sister's husband's brother."

Ramose couldn't help wondering if a man who was cross-eyed would make a good soldier, but he kept his thoughts to himself.

"We're joining a unit that is going to sail over the Great Green to conquer the eastern lands."

Karoya was horrified at the thought of sailing on the sea.

"I've heard that sometimes the boat goes so far out to sea that you can't see the shore." Karoya's eyes were wide. "That can't be true, can it?" she asked.

"It's true," said Hori. "And sometimes the waves rise up to the height of three men."

"Why are you going to do this?" said Karoya. "Why don't you stay on land where it's safe?"

"We were working in the alabaster quarries in the south. It's hard work. I heard that Pharaoh, may he have long life and health, was recruiting for the navy. My friends and I thought we'd give it a try."

Ramose couldn't quite put his finger on it, but there was something he didn't like about Hori and his friends. Perhaps it was the way one of Hori's eyes always seemed to be on him.

They made good progress. "At this rate we'll be in Memphis in two days," said Hapu the next day.

Hapu had been in a very cheerful mood ever since they'd come on board. He chatted happily to Hori, telling them all about the work on Pharaoh's tomb.

"It's supposed to be a secret, Hapu," said Ramose wishing his friend was grumpy and silent again, instead of happy and talkative.

"I haven't said where the tomb is," said Hapu. "And anyway it's destroyed now."

Ramose was starting to get nervous about arriving in Memphis. He had begun to think that he would never regain his place as heir to Egypt's throne, never see his father, never become pharaoh. Suddenly, in two days, he would be able to contact his sister again and see his sick father.

Now that the wait was over, the thought of arriving in Memphis quite scared him. His plan for actually getting inside the palace there was rather vague. He decided that the best thing to do was to find his sister first, but how he would get to her without the vizier knowing he hadn't yet worked out.

Hori came and sat beside him.

"You are a scribe, I see," said Hori looking with one eye at the palette and pen box in Ramose's bag.

"An apprentice scribe," said Ramose.

"That's a nice set of scribal tools," said Hori.

"I inherited it from my previous master, who died in the flood," lied Ramose closing his bag. He was conscious that the ebony palette inlaid with gold, ivory and turquoise was far too rich for an apprentice scribe to own.

"Tell me what you make of this," Hori said pulling a very old-looking piece of papyrus from his own bag.

Ramose noticed that it had a royal seal, though the blob of wax was cracking with age. He unrolled the papyrus and read the flowing script.

"It's instructions," he said.

"Instructions on how to get inside a pyramid?" asked Intef.

Seth thumped him in the chest to silence him.

"No," replied Ramose. "Instructions on how to lead a good life and attain knowledge. I've read many texts like this. My tutor made me copy them out endlessly."

He turned over the scroll. "There is mention of a pyramid, the pyramid of one of the old pharaohs."

The three men leaned forward. "Does it say anything about the tomb within the pyramid?"

"It could be about the location of a tomb, but it's written like a puzzle, a riddle, as if the person who wrote it didn't really want anyone to find it. Where did you get it from?"

"Oh, I just picked it up somewhere," Hori said vaguely. Intef and Seth, who had hardly spoken since they'd been aboard, started whispering to each other. "I'll hand it in to the authorities when we get to Memphis."

They tied up in the afternoon. "Why are we stopping so early?" asked Hapu. "We usually keep going till sunset."

"This is a good place to moor for the night," said the captain. "Further up, the river bank is rocky and it's more difficult to get ashore."

The soldiers set up their camp on shore near some pretty farming land. Some of them used the extra daylight hours to wash their kilts at the river's edge. Others fished with their spears. Karoya helped the cook collect fuel for the cooking fire.

Hapu leaned back comfortably on a ridge of sand. "I shall almost miss this life."

"Make the most of it, you could be in prison this time tomorrow," said Ramose in a low voice. "Arrested for breaking into the palace."

"Don't be so gloomy. It's too nice a day."

The sun was setting and the sky turned pale orange. It was a nice day, but Ramose couldn't help but worry about what might be ahead of them.

They had a pleasant meal of ox meat, newly baked bread and vegetables. After dinner the soldiers played senet and a rather childish ball game. Hapu joined in enthusiastically.

Ramose laid out his reed mat away from the soldiers where it was quieter. The others eventually settled down to sleep, but Ramose lay awake looking at the stars. He couldn't sleep. Hapu was snoring softly. Karoya was sleeping under her head shawl. All the soldiers were asleep as well. The only other creature awake was Mery who was trying to settle down on Ramose's stomach. Ramose had pushed the cat away at least half a dozen times, but it kept coming back, digging its claws into his chest. Ramose sat up abruptly and grabbed the cat. He stuffed it into his reed bag.

"Now perhaps you'll go to sleep and leave me alone," hissed Ramose.

He tied a leather thong around the opening. The bag was loosely woven, the cat would be able to breathe easily enough. He lay down again with a sigh.

Just as Ramose was starting to drift off to sleep, he felt a hand clamp over his mouth. It was a dirty, sweaty hand that smelt of onions. Ramose tried to pull it off, but other hands turned him over roughly and tied his arms behind his back.

A gag was tied tightly over his mouth. Ramose fought furiously against his bindings but he couldn't break free. A short, dark figure hauled him to his feet and forced him to walk away from his friends and into the darkness. He struggled against his captors. They muttered and cursed him. Something cracked him on the head.

6

KIDNAPPED

SOMEONE was slapping his face. It hurt. His whole head hurt. "Come on, wake up," said a rough voice. It was Hori. "Intef's tired of carrying you."

Ramose was lying on the ground. Hori was leaning over him. He slapped him again. Ramose tried to sit up, but he couldn't because his hands were tied behind him. His jaw was stiff and sore.

His mouth was dry because of the tight gag. He rolled onto his side. Ramose didn't know where he was. It was still dark. He couldn't hear the sound of the river, but the air was still moist and he could feel grass beneath him. Hori and Intef were watching him. Seth was opening Ramose's bag. He undid the string. There was a ferocious spitting and hissing as Mery leapt out of the bag. Seth shrieked. Mery darted off into the darkness.

"It's a monster," Seth yelled. "The boy's got a monster in his bag."

Ramose would have laughed if he hadn't had a strip of linen gagging him. He hoped the cat could find its way back to Karoya.

"It was the slave girl's cat, stupid," said Hori. "Let's get moving. We've got a long way to go before it gets light."

Ramose's moment of pleasure disappeared as Intef dragged him to his feet. After walking for about two hours in the dark, the moon rose. Ramose could see two pyramids in the distance, their limestone faces gave off a soft glow in the moonlight. They were walking towards the larger pyramid. It was surrounded by tombs, chapels and temples. As they got closer, Ramose could see that there was a row of trees planted around the edge of the pyramid. There were not only date palms and tamarisks, but also sacred persea trees.

It was starting to get light by now. Ramose was tired. He could tell the other men were as well, but Hori was making them hurry. He led them to a crumbling rectangular tomb where he broke open the door and they went inside just as the sun rose. Inside was a chapel with painted walls. Ramose knew that somewhere below them an important person would be buried.

"No one goes outside until it's dark again," said Hori laying down his reed mat.

"I don't like the idea of sleeping in a tomb," said Seth looking nervously in all the dark corners.

Intef's brow furrowed. "What if I want to…"

"Go now," said Hori. "Seth, you go out and find a temple that's still in use and steal some of the food offerings."

"Do I have to?"

"Yes."

Seth left reluctantly. He soon returned with food and the robbers feasted on the meat, vegetables and sweet cakes that he had stolen from a temple. When they had finished eating, Hori belched loudly.

"Untie the scribe's hands." He nodded to Seth who went over and untied the rope around Ramose's wrists.

They gave him a piece of dry bread and a few mouthfuls of warm beer.

"Intef, you sleep in front of the door," Hori said

as he settled himself down. "Just in case the scribe decides to wander off." He grinned at Seth. "Or in case any spirits try and get us."

They were all asleep within a few minutes. All except for Ramose. He couldn't sleep. Seth had insisted on leaving a lamp burning. In the dim light, Ramose looked at the paintings on the walls of the chapel. He peered at the writing. It was the tomb of a priest called Amenhotep. There was a painting of the priest and his wife, ploughing in the Field of Reeds in the afterlife. Another painting showed the couple praising Osiris. The third wall had a scene from Amenhotep's funeral. The fourth wall showed a banquet with girls dancing and playing musical instruments. In the dim light it reminded Ramose of the palace and his own room with its wall paintings. There was an offering table, but it looked like it had been a very long time since anyone had brought offerings for Amenhotep.

Ramose felt like he'd only just got to sleep when Seth was shaking him awake again.

"Come on, Scribe," he said. "You've got work to do."

Breakfast was another mouthful of dry bread, and three dates. Ramose suspected it was nowhere near breakfast time.

"I'm thirsty."

Hori gave him a flask of beer.

"Don't you have any water?" Ramose asked.

"No."

Outside it was a still, cool evening. It was peaceful. Nothing disturbed the quiet but the howling of a distant dog, the buzzing of insects and Intef's heavy breathing. Ramose thought that many people probably worked in the area, tending the tombs and the temples around the pyramids. There was no one around, though. All the workers had returned to their homes for the night. Ramose was led by his captors towards the pyramid, which loomed eerily in the dark.

"Okay, Scribe," said Hori. "This is where you earn your keep."

"Since you've only given me a piece of dry bread and three dates, there can't be much for me to do."

"Don't get smart," said Hori pulling out the papyrus that he had shown Ramose on the boat. "Find the entrance to the tomb."

Ramose had guessed that the men were tomb robbers. He hated the idea of helping them, but at that moment he didn't think that he had a choice. He peered at the papyrus in the dim light of an oil lamp. "It says:

Read these words well, they will teach you.

If you disturb the great one's place of rest, you will feel the wrath of the gods.

If riches come to you by theft, they will not stay the night with you.

The greedy man will have no tomb.

He will be tortured for eternity by the spirits."

"Maybe this isn't such a good idea," said Seth, glancing around nervously.

"Don't worry about that stuff. It's just to scare us off," Hori said. "Get to the important bit. Where's the tomb entrance?"

Ramose read on.

"Seek the truth where you least expect it,"

"What's that supposed to mean?" asked Intef, his brow furrowed with confusion.

"Tomb entrances are always facing north, aren't they?" said Hori. "Aligned with certain stars."

Ramose nodded.

"So maybe the entrance is on the south face of the pyramid," said Seth.

Hori nodded. "Yes but where? What else does it say, Scribe?"

"It says:

The sun rises twenty and seven cubits from the east and climbs to a height of ten and five cubits."

"That must be the measurements to find the entrance," said Hori.

Ramose was sure he was right, but he didn't say anything. He was thinking about what the scroll had said about feeling the wrath of the gods. The tomb robbers were hurrying to the south side of the pyramid. Ramose reluctantly followed them.

The men measured out the distances that Ramose read out from the papyrus. Intef clambered up the side of the pyramid with the aid of a rickety ladder that they made out of tamarisk branches and reeds. Intef had a large stone hammer tied around his waist.

"There's no sign of a doorway," said Intef.

"Of course there isn't," snapped Hori. "It's a hidden entrance!"

"Are you sure this is where it is?"

"Twenty and seven cubits from the eastern corner. Ten and five cubits up the side, that's what it says isn't it, boy?"

Ramose nodded, feeling a wave of guilt at helping the criminals.

Intef took the hammer from his belt and with a mighty swing smashed it into the side of the pyramid. The sound seemed deafeningly loud in the quiet of the evening. Ramose winced. The robbers listened anxiously to see if the noise had attracted anyone.

"It hardly made a mark," said Intef.

"It's solid stone," said Seth impatiently. "It's

going to take more than one whack to break it."

Intef swung the hammer again and again. It took a dozen blows before the stone block even cracked. It looked like the ladder might give way before he broke it. The big man continued to swing the hammer, grunting louder with the exertion of each blow. His body glistened in the moonlight as the sweat ran down him.

"This is getting nowhere," he called down.

"That's because you're useless," Hori shouted. "Do I have to come up and do it myself?"

Even though Intef was plainly stupid, he didn't like anybody saying so. He swung his hammer with a growl of anger. The stone exploded under the blow, pieces of rock showered down on those watching below.

"That's more like it," said Hori with an ugly grin, aware that his jibe had worked.

"Don't get too excited," said Intef. "There's another layer underneath that one."

"Well, you better get into it, otherwise it'll be daybreak and we'll still be on the outside."

The second layer was thicker but made of mud brick. With a lot of grumbling and a few more hefty blows, Intef's hammer disappeared inside the pyramid. Seth cheered.

"Shut up, you fool," said Hori. "We don't want to bring the temple guards over here. Get the lamps and the bag, Scribe. You're going in with him."

"What about you?"

"Seth and I will keep watch."

Seth smiled, relieved that he didn't have to go inside the pyramid. It was an ugly sight as the robber had hardly any teeth. Ramose tentatively put his foot on the shaky ladder and climbed to the hole, balancing an oil lamp in one hand and with a bag of tools over his shoulder.

The air from inside the tomb was cool and had a strange smell. It was escaping after being sealed inside for four centuries. While he had been waiting for Intef to break into the pyramid, he'd read the papyrus carefully. The pyramid contained the tomb of Pharaoh Senusret from long ago.

Ramose remembered the name from Keneben's lists of kings, which he'd had to learn off by heart back in the palace schoolroom. He crawled in through the hole gouged in the white limestone of the pyramid. He'd been a good pharaoh as far as Ramose could remember, known for irrigation systems and trade with foreigners. Ramose didn't like the idea of disturbing his tomb.

THE SECRETS OF THE PYRAMID

INSIDE THE PYRAMID a narrow passage sloped downwards. The walls were lined with plain limestone, not decorated with carvings as his father's tomb had been. He sighed. He should be on his way to his father now, not stumbling around inside a pyramid. He could see Intef ahead, with a coil of rope over one shoulder and the stone hammer swinging from his waist. The ceiling was low and the big man had to stoop. So this is what it feels like to be a tomb robber, Ramose thought to himself. He had always found it hard to believe such people really existed. People who were so greedy for gold that they were willing to risk severe punishments. He'd heard of tomb robbers having their ears and lips cut off. More often than not they were executed. And that was only in this world. In the afterlife, tomb robbers faced eternal oblivion. No growing wheat in the Fields of Reeds for them. He wondered how Osiris, the god of the underworld, would judge an unwilling tomb robber.

Ramose had been expecting to feel his usual fear of enclosed spaces, but he didn't. Perhaps it was because it was night, and the darkness inside the pyramid seemed like a continuation of the darkness outside. Perhaps it was because he was tired and hungry. He hadn't seen any daylight for two days. He felt as if everything that was happening wasn't real, as if it was a dream and therefore nothing to be afraid of. As he descended into the depths of the pyramid he felt a strange calmness, as if he was watching himself from somewhere else—somewhere where it was safe.

At the bottom of the sloping shaft there was a high-ceilinged chamber. Intef straightened up with a groan. He looked around, squinting in the dim light of his lamp. The chamber had been carefully lined with smooth limestone, but it was completely empty.

"Where's the sarcophagus?" he said.

Ramose smiled at the man's stupidity. "If it was that easy to find the actual burial chamber it would have been robbed ages ago."

Intef's brow creased.

"The architect who built this didn't want the tomb to be found. He probably designed it with hidden passages and dead-end tunnels. There could be traps."

"But you know all about it from the writing, don't you?"

"It's written in a sort of riddle."

Intef walked around the chamber feeling the solid limestone walls. "But there's no other way out of this room."

"Yes there is," said Ramose who was beginning to enjoy making Intef look foolish, which wasn't hard. He read from the papyrus.

"Allow thy soul to be raised up towards heaven.

This is the best and shortest road towards knowledge.

The way of knowledge is narrow.

You must become a low and creeping thing."

Intef stood with his head cocked on one side like a large and stupid dog.

Ramose held his lamp above his head. The

roof of the chamber was made of stepped slabs of stone so that it narrowed to a point.

"The entrance to the next tunnel must be up there somewhere."

Intef held his lamp up and looked up. With the light from both lamps they could just make out a small dark square. It was at least the height of four men above them.

"How will we get up there?" asked Intef.

Ramose shrugged. "Don't ask me, I'm just a scribe."

They went back up the entrance shaft and pulled up the ladder. Even with the ladder in place underneath the upper tunnel entrance, it was still well short. Intef roughly carved handholds in the stone as far as he could reach from the top of the ladder. Greed had made him fearless. He climbed up, gripping the holes he had gouged in the limestone wall. Ramose was expecting him to slip and fall at every moment. He didn't. The big man clambered up the sheer wall like an enormous spider. He reached a ledge and crawled onto it.

"Okay, Scribe," he said. "Your turn."

"But I'm shorter than you, I won't be able to reach the handholds you've made."

Ramose felt the end of a coil of rope drop on his head.

"Tie that around you," said Intef.

Ramose tied the rope securely around his waist and then climbed the ladder. When he reached the top, he felt himself being lifted into the air. Intef hauled him up as if he was a sack of grain, not worrying about how he banged against the stone. Ramose grabbed hold of the ledge and clambered up onto it. A new passage sloped up from the ledge they were standing on in the direction of the centre of the pyramid. It had a low ceiling, nothing more than a tunnel roughly carved through solid stone.

"You go first," said Intef.

Ramose knew it was pointless to argue. He got down on his hands and knees and started to crawl up the tunnel, like a creeping thing, just as the papyrus had foretold. He held his oil lamp in one hand; it was no easy task. Ramose could hear Intef complaining as he crawled along behind.

Ramose's calm began to fade. He suspected his lack of fear had only been the effect of the beer on an empty stomach. He was now starting to imagine the hundreds of mud bricks just above his head. The narrowness of the tomb was making him feel stifled. He kept crawling. He thought about his friends. He wondered what they had done when they woke up and found him gone. They had no gold or copper to exchange for food. He began to think that he'd misread the papyrus, that this was a blind tunnel leading nowhere. He wanted to turn around and crawl back out again, but he knew the tunnel would be blocked by Intef's sweaty body. Even if the robber wanted to, he couldn't turn around in the narrow tunnel.

Just when Ramose was starting to really panic, the tunnel came to an end. He emerged in a passage which ran at right angles to the tunnel. This passage was wider, higher and properly faced with smooth limestone. Ramose stood up and straightened his aching back with relief. Intef came crawling out of the tunnel, cursing the workmen who made it so narrow. He stood up and peered down the new passage.

"The burial chamber must be this way," he said walking eagerly down the passage.

"Wait," said Ramose. "Don't be in such a hurry." He studied the papyrus and read aloud.

"Woe unto the impatient man. The goddess of the celestial ocean draws you down to her waters."

"Oh, that's just flowery writing," said Intef as he hurried on down the passage. "Don't take..."

Intef stopped suddenly. He stood frozen. Ramose came up behind him and held out his lamp. Intef was standing on the edge of a vertical shaft. The toes of his sandals were hanging over the edge. The shaft was only two cubits across, but it was too wide to jump safely to the other side. Ramose could not see how deep it was. He picked up a small stone and dropped it. He waited. After what seemed like minutes, he heard a faint splash. He looked at Intef. The big man had a terrified look on his face, realising that he had very nearly plunged to his death.

"Don't bother to thank me," Ramose said.

Intef found his voice. "How do we get across?" he asked shakily.

Ramose walked back along the passage looking for something that would span the gap. He found a recess in the limestone wall and a plank of wood that a lazy tomb maker had left there centuries earlier. He looked at it doubtfully. He didn't know whether he was prepared to trust his weight to a four hundred-year-old plank. He didn't have any choice.

"Hurry up," Intef prodded Ramose in the back. "We must be close to the burial chamber now."

Ramose lowered the plank over the gap. Intef loaded him up with the coil of rope and the bag of tools. He put his foot on the plank. He was glad he couldn't see the drop. He took one tentative step. The plank creaked. He took another step and it sagged in the middle. Ramose took two more steps, his heart racing, and he was over. Intef looked across at him.

"I don't know if it'll hold your weight," Ramose said. "Why don't I go on ahead and see if it's worth the risk?"

"Oh, no you don't." Intef didn't trust Ramose. "You could pocket half the gold."

"Okay. Come across then."

The big man took a breath and ran towards the gaping shaft. His full weight hit the middle of the plank. It cracked. He lunged forward as the ancient wood broke. He grasped hold of the rock ledge on the other side, his legs dangling down into the shaft. His feet scrabbled on the rock face but couldn't find anything that would support him. His hands clawed at the ledge. He started to slip.

"Help me," shouted Intef, his voice was high pitched with fear.

Ramose heard the broken pieces of plank hit the water far below with a faint splash. It seemed like they'd been falling for hours. He watched Intef's big, ugly hands grasping at the rock. For a split second, he thought about pushing the robber into the shaft, but instead he reached out and grabbed Intef under the arms. The man found a rock protrusion with his foot and levered himself up. Ramose hauled him onto the ledge.

"You knew that wouldn't hold my weight," grumbled Intef as he got to his feet.

Ramose was looking down into the shaft and wondering how they would get back over it again.

Intef's lamp bowl had broken when he fell, so they now had only one lamp between them. They walked along the passage which was sloping down slightly until it suddenly divided into two. Ramose held the lamp up to the papyrus scroll.

"The next bit is torn," he said. "I don't know which is the right passage."

"We'll take this one," said Intef. "You go first."

Ramose entered the right-hand passage. It twisted and turned. Up until then, Ramose had been able to keep a picture in his head of the way they had come. He'd still had a sense of which way north lay and where the burial chamber should be. After the passage had made six or more turns, he had no idea which way he was facing. The oil in the lamp was running low. Intef topped it up from a jar in his bag. They followed the passage for another three turns. Then it ended abruptly.

"You did that on purpose, didn't you?" said Intef. "You knew this was the wrong passage."

Ramose wasn't listening. He was sniffing.

"Can you smell something?"

He felt a burning in his throat. He looked down at his feet. They were almost buried in a fine yellow powder which covered the floor. Clouds of the powder had been kicked up as they'd walked around.

Ramose put his hand over his mouth and ran back along the passage. Intef followed him. Ramose felt dizzy. When he reached the fork in the passage he vomited. Intef was looking ill.

"What was that?" said Intef, taking a swig of his water. The big man's face had a greenish colour in the dim light.

Ramose retched again. "It must have been some sort of poison."

Intef reluctantly handed his water container to Ramose.

They retraced their steps and took the other passage which sloped down at a greater angle. Ramose thought they must now be down below ground level. He was still feeling sick and dizzy, but he hoped the poison had lost its potency over the centuries. The passage twisted and turned just as the other one had. Suddenly it opened into a chamber. It was exactly the same as the first chamber they had entered, high-ceilinged, lined with limestone—and completely empty.

Intef threw the coil of rope onto the floor. "You've led me astray again!"

Ramose sat down groggily. "Why would I do that? My father is dying in Memphis. I just want to get out of here."

Intef took another swig of water.

"This looks like the burial chamber," Ramose said looking around in the dim light. "Look at how smooth the limestone on the walls is. And see that niche?" He held the lamp over to one side lighting a recess cut into the wall. "That's where the Canopic chest would fit."

"So what are you saying?" said Intef chewing on a piece of dried meat. "They went to all the trouble of building this pyramid and then didn't use it?"

"That's a possibility. It might be nothing more than a giant hoax to lure tomb robbers away from the real tomb which is hidden somewhere else."

"What a dirty trick!" said Intef, spitting out bits of dried ox flesh.

Ramose didn't really believe that was the case at all. He didn't want the robbers to get the old pharaoh's gold and jewels. He thought about trying to convince Intef that the pyramid was empty, but he knew Hori wouldn't let him go until they found some treasure. If the tomb robbers didn't find it in the pyramid, they would have him digging holes all around it, looking for secret tombs. He had to get this over and done with so that he could get to Memphis and see his father. Ramose stood up again and walked around the chamber, looking closely at the walls and the ceiling in the dim light of the oil lamp. He studied the papyrus again. There had to be a clue.

The nut doesn't reveal the tree it contains.
The ignorant man doesn't see the truth
Though he treads upon it with his sandals.

Ramose dropped down onto his hands and knees and set the lamp on the stone floor. He ran his hands over it as if he was looking for something small that he'd lost. Intef looked as confused as ever.

"Here," said Ramose. He'd found what he was looking for. "Bring the lever over here."

For once, Intef didn't argue. He took a lever made of hardwood from his bag.

"There's a gap here. See?" Ramose brushed the dust away and ran his fingers around in a square. "It's a trapdoor."

8

THE DEAD PHARAOH

THE LEVER was too thick to fit into the groove. Intef, impatient to get to the gold that he was sure was inside the tomb, got out his stone hammer and started to bash the slab of stone. The slab was thinner than the one that had covered the entrance to the pyramid. It was also horizontal, which made it easier for Intef to let the weight of the hammer do all the work. The slab soon cracked, then it broke into several pieces which disappeared from view and crashed to another floor not far below.

Ramose held the lamp down. The light reflected off gold in all corners of a chamber. Intef eagerly lowered himself down the hole, falling awkwardly on the floor three cubits below.

"This is it!" he exclaimed, limping around the chamber. "Look at all this!"

Ramose peered down the hole. He didn't know whether to be pleased or not. At one end of the chamber was a huge red granite sarcophagus. It was five cubits in length and three cubits high. All around the room there were chests covered with gold foil and pieces of furniture inlaid with jewels. Intef pushed a chest under the hole and balanced an elegantly carved chair inlaid with turquoise on top of it.

"Get down here with that lamp," he ordered.

Ramose clambered down. Intef was flinging open the lids of chests, laughing and exclaiming over all the jewellery, bowls and goblets he found within them. His face shone with the light reflecting from all the gold.

"This is just the beginning," he said turning to the sarcophagus.

"Can't we just take this stuff and leave the pharaoh in peace?" pleaded Ramose. "There's enough here to keep the three of you rich for the rest of your lives. More than enough. You don't need any more treasure."

Intef wasn't listening. He was trying to lift the lid from the sarcophagus. It was obviously impossible. The lid was made of solid granite two palm-widths thick. He pushed its edge with all his might.

"You can't push it off, Intef," said Ramose. "It'll be fitted inside the sarcophagus. You'll have to lift it."

Intef had another idea though. He climbed back up the hole and brought down his stone hammer. With a loud grunt he swung the hammer as high as he could and brought it down on the lid with all his strength. Ramose thought of the long-dead tomb makers and all the trouble they'd gone to in order to keep their pharaoh's resting place secret. They had built his sarcophagus with skill and care. It wasn't going to give up its treasure easily.

Intef continued to swing his hammer at the lid. He broke off a corner. Encouraged by this he smashed the hammer down on the broken edge. Intef furiously rained blows on the corner of the sarcophagus. Ramose sat on a chest and watched. He couldn't help thinking that if Intef used all that energy on something constructive, he'd be a lot better off. Eventually, after more than half an hour, the big tomb robber stopped and rested his hammer on the floor. He was gasping for breath and sweat was running down his back. There was a jagged hole in the end of the sarcophagus lid.

"That should do it," panted Intef.

Ramose looked puzzled. "You still won't be able to lift it off."

"I won't have to." Intef smiled unpleasantly. "You're going to get inside and bring everything out."

Ramose looked at the hole with horror. It was just about big enough for him to wriggle through. "I can't go in there," he said, starting to sweat despite the cool air of the tomb. "I...I'm not very good in enclosed spaces."

"Too bad." Intef lifted Ramose up and put him on top of the sarcophagus as if he was no heavier than a handful of figs. "Get on with it. We've got to get out of here before daylight."

Ramose threaded his legs in through the hole in the granite sarcophagus. His feet rested on the coffin. Ramose opened his mouth, and then closed it again. He knew there was no point in arguing.

"Give me the lamp."

Intef handed him the lamp. Ramose took a deep breath and lowered himself into the sarcophagus. The coffin was large and roughly human-shaped. It was decorated with beautiful patterns and a painting of the sky-goddess Nut with her wings outspread. Even in the dim lamplight, Ramose could see that the colours were as bright as if they were newly painted. He found it hard to believe that the coffin was four hundred years old. There was just enough room for Ramose to straddle the foot of the coffin.

"Do you want this?" asked Intef pushing the hammer through the hole.

"No," said Ramose. "I don't have to break it open. I can get the lid off."

It wasn't that easy though. He tried to get his fingers under the lid. It was jammed on tight. The carpenters who had made the wooden coffin had made the lid a perfect fit. They had never intended that anyone would be opening it.

"We haven't got time, just smash it open." Intef was getting impatient.

"Just let me try with a chisel first."

Intef handed him a chisel and Ramose fitted it in the crack between the lid and the base of the coffin. He wriggled it up and down, making the crack wider.

"Hurry up."

Ramose eventually eased the lid off. It parted from the coffin base with a sigh. Ramose pushed the lid over to one side.

The first thing he noticed was the smell. It smelt just like the embalming room under the temple where he had woken up after his nanny and tutor had faked his death. It was the strong resinous smell of juniper oil and frankincense.

He held up the lamp. Inside the coffin was the pharaoh's mummy. A gilded mask stared up at him with blank eyes. The pharaoh's face had a strong nose and a mouth that was almost smiling. He'd always imagined mummies bound in soft white linen strips, but the bandages on the mummy in front of him were brown with age and stiff with the oils, long since dried up, that the priests had poured onto it during the burial ritual.

"Are there jewels? Is there gold?"

"Yes."

Ramose's lamplight reflected on a magnificent gold collar draped around the neck of the mummy and a gold crown on its head. The collar was made of hundreds, maybe thousands of beads of turquoise, carnelian, lapis lazuli and gold.

Ramose hesitated for a moment. Would he suffer the fate of a tomb robber if he was caught? And what about in the afterlife? Would Osiris understand that he'd had no choice? He pulled the collar from the mummy. The beautiful pattern disintegrated and the beads cascaded into the bottom of the coffin.

"What's going on in there?"

"The threads stringing the beads are rotten. Give me a bag."

Ramose scooped up beads by the handful and put them into the bag that Intef handed him.

The threads of the armbands broke as well. He scooped those beads into the bag with the others. Then he took off the crown. It was solid gold with a snake's head inlaid with turquoise rearing from the front as if to attack anyone who dared harm the pharaoh. Intef thrust a sharpened flint through the hole.

"Cut open the bandages. There'll be amulets wrapped inside."

Ramose didn't argue. He slit the bandages binding the mummy down the front and peeled them back. Sure enough there were exquisite amulets made of gold and precious stones. There was a heart scarab of lapis lazuli, similar to his own.

"Check the hands as well. There should be rings."

Ramose slit open the linen strips binding the hands to get to the dead pharaoh's fingers. The skin was like dried-out leather. The fingers were like black claws. Each one had at least one ring on it. As Ramose hurried to get the jewels, one of the fingers broke off in his hand. Until then, Ramose hadn't had time to think about his fear of enclosed spaces. Touching the actual withered flesh of the dead pharaoh made his stomach lurch and his heart pound. He was suddenly aware that he was inside a stone tomb, straddling a dead man. Above him was a mountain of stone and mud bricks. The fumes of the embalming resins were making his head spin. He threw the bag out of the hole and scrambled to get out of the sarcophagus.

"What's the rush all of a sudden?"

"Got to get outside."

Intef grabbed him by the arm and took the lamp from him, setting it down safely on the lid of the sarcophagus. "You're not going anywhere yet."

Ramose tried to struggle out of Intef's grasp. "I can't breathe. I need air. Fresh air. I have to get out."

Intef slapped him hard on the face with the back of his hand. "We're not leaving until we've gone through these chests."

Intef opened all the chests one by one and took out everything of value.

Ramose's breathing slowed. He wouldn't get out of the pyramid if he panicked. If Intef hadn't slapped him, he might have gone charging up the passage, fallen down the shaft and drowned in the celestial waters, or taken a wrong turn and ended up back in the poisonous yellow powder.

"Now get up to the upper chamber and I'll hand this all to you."

It was a slow business, but at the sight of the treasure Intef's impatience had completely disappeared. He handed the items one by one to

Ramose, up through the hole in the ceiling of the burial chamber. Ramose, in the darkness of the upper chamber had no choice but to do as he was told.

"We'll need something to make a bridge across the gap as well," Intef looked around the chamber. There was a tall shrine in one corner of the chamber. It had two doors covered with delicately patterned gold foil. Inside was a wooden statue of the goddess Hathor. Intef grabbed hold of one of the doors and ripped it from its hinges. Ramose winced at the destruction of such a beautiful thing. He handed that up to Ramose as well. Finally Intef came up himself with the lamp.

There were four sacks of treasure. Intef carried three and gave one to Ramose to carry. They retraced their steps. Laying the shrine door across the shaft, they crossed the dark space. Then they crawled through the tunnel, Intef hauling his three sacks behind him.

It seemed to take forever. Ramose just kept thinking of the air and the space outside. Every step he took, every finger-width he crawled, brought him closer to it. He followed the dim light and Intef's grunts. The smell of the robber's sweating body just in front of him made him retch, but he kept going. Eventually they reached the end of the tunnel and climbed down to the false burial chamber. As he walked up the final passage, Ramose saw a dark blue square ahead of them, tinged with pink. It was the entrance to the passage. It was almost daybreak.

Hori and Seth were waiting impatiently.

"What took you so long?" called Hori as Intef thrust the ladder out of the hole in the pyramid and climbed down it.

Intef didn't say anything but threw down the four sacks of treasure. Ramose could hear the greedy sounds of the men gloating over their haul as he climbed down the rickety ladder. His legs were trembling. He was exhausted, parched and hungry. He collapsed on the ground.

"We had a visitor while you were away," said Hori with a smirk.

Ramose realised there was another figure in the group. Someone with his hands and feet tied. It was Hapu.

9

THE TOMB OF THE PRINCESS

T HE TOMB ROBBERS took their treasure and their prisoners back to the hiding place in the abandoned tomb. While Hori and Seth were poring over the pharaoh's treasure, Ramose sat with Hapu. Hori was so pleased with the haul that he'd given Ramose some dry bread and fish to eat. Ramose was still feeling sick, but he ate some of the food.

"I didn't know what to think when I woke up and you were gone," said Hapu. Now that they were back inside the temple, the tomb robbers had untied him.

"You thought I'd gone on to Memphis without you?"

"It did cross my mind, but when Karoya found that Mery was missing, she was convinced something was wrong."

"I would never have left you without food."

"That's what Karoya said. And no boats would have passed during the night, so we knew you must have gone inland."

"How did you find out where I was?"

"A boy minding pigs told us he'd heard the sound of men swearing during the night and Karoya found some footprints in the sand so we knew which direction you'd taken. Once we saw the pyramids, we guessed that's where they'd be heading. I wanted to search the temples. Karoya thought they'd be more interested in the tombs." Hapu looked guilty. "We had an argument. She went towards the pyramids and I started searching the temples. Hori saw me and captured me last night."

"So Karoya doesn't know where you are?"

"No."

Their conversation was interrupted by the sound of eerie wailing coming from just outside the tomb door. Seth looked up from the treasure in fear.

"What was that?"

"Just some sort of wild animal," said Hori.

"It sounds like a ghost to me, Seth," said Ramose.

Hapu smiled grimly. "What are we going to do?" he whispered to Ramose.

Ramose sighed. They had to get away from the tomb robbers. He knew he had to come up with a plan, but his mind wasn't working. He hadn't slept for two nights and he couldn't think straight.

"I have to get some sleep," he said to Hapu. He wrapped his cloak around him and lay down.

When Ramose awoke, the tomb robbers were preparing for another robbery.

"There are other tombs close to the pyramid," Hori said to Ramose.

"It doesn't say anything about other tombs on the papyrus," said Ramose trying to put Hori off. The last thing he wanted was to have to go down into another tomb.

"I found the entrance to one yesterday while you were in the pyramid. You wouldn't lie to me about what's in the papyrus, would you?"

"No. I told you, the papyrus is just about the pyramid."

"Well, you and your friend are going down into

this tomb anyway, just as soon as it gets dark."

"You better let us out of here immediately," said Hapu. "You don't realise who Ramose really is."

"He's an apprentice scribe," said Intef looking puzzled.

"No he isn't. That's just a disguise," replied Hapu. "He's Prince Ramose, Pharaoh's son."

"I'm not stupid, you know," said Intef. "Prince Ramose died last year, everyone knows that."

"We were thinking of robbing his tomb, but there were still too many people in the valley," said Hori.

"He didn't really die. It was all a trick. This is him."

Hori nodded. "I'm actually a vizier. Did you know that? And Intef is a high priest. We're all in disguise."

The tomb robbers all laughed at the joke. Seth suddenly let out a yell.

"There's a rat in the food bag," he said throwing the bag across the room.

"Is it alive?" asked Intef.

"I think it's dead."

Hori went over and prodded the bag. He opened it cautiously with a stick. Inside the bag among the temple offerings that they had stolen, was a dead rat.

"It must have been poisoned by the tomb bread," said Intef.

"It didn't die of poisoning. Something has killed it. See? It's bleeding."

The rat was still limp and bleeding from a wound in the neck.

"Do spirits have teeth?" asked Seth anxiously.

"Don't worry about it. Let's get going."

Intef grumbled all the way to the pyramid. "I'm not going down into another tomb. I hurt my ankle last night."

When they reached the pyramid, they walked around to the western side. Beyond the wall around the pyramid, outside the row of trees, there was an untended rocky area. Hori and Seth went over to a pile of rocks and started throwing them aside.

"Don't just stand there," Hori said to Ramose and Hapu. "Help." He turned to Intef. "You too."

They moved the pile of rocks and underneath they found a flat stone slab. Hori handed Intef the lever and the big man lifted the slab and pulled it aside.

Ramose smelt the same strange smell of ancient air as he had at the pyramid. He held up a lamp and looked down the shaft. It was a sheer drop.

"There's no ramp," he said. "The shaft's at least sixty cubits deep. How will you get down?"

"I'm not going down," said Hori. "You two are."

Hapu looked alarmed. "By ourselves?"

"No, don't worry, I'll send Seth down to hold your hand."

Seth didn't look happy. "Do I have to go down?"

"Intef's hurt his ankle. It's your turn to go down."

Ramose didn't bother arguing. He slung the bag containing tools and lamp oil over his shoulder. Intef tied the rope around Ramose's waist. The big man took a firm hold of the rope and braced himself. He nodded to Ramose. Ramose heard Hapu gasp as he stepped out into the dark hole, trusting the weight of his body to Intef's strong hands. He swung free. The big tomb robber grunted as he slowly lowered Ramose down the shaft. As he descended into the coolness of the tomb, Ramose felt the same dreamlike calm come over him as he had when he had entered the pyramid. He was getting used to being in tombs. It was almost as if he preferred them. He hadn't seen daylight in three days. He'd forgotten what it was like. Darkness was normal.

Hapu was lowered down next and then Seth. The boys held out their lamps to see what was around them.

"What do you see?" Hori's voice echoed down the shaft.

"Is there gold?" Intef shouted eagerly.

"There's just a tunnel," Seth shouted back.

"We'll see where it leads." He started forward and then changed his mind. "You go first," he said.

The boys walked slowly along the tunnel. It was a rough-hewn passage, but not as low as the tunnel in the pyramid. Ramose and Hapu could walk along it comfortably, if they bent their heads a little. Seth had to bend over double.

"We better watch out for those demons you read about," said Hapu.

"What demons?" said Seth trying to look in front of him and behind him at the same time.

"He's just joking, Seth," said Ramose. "There was nothing about demons on the papyrus."

A noise echoed down the tunnel, the sound of falling rocks.

"What was that?" said Seth. He was so afraid, he almost grabbed Ramose's arm.

"It was just some stones falling down the shaft."

"It sounded like it was coming from the tunnel."

"It's an illusion. The sound echoes from one wall to another."

"I'm not so sure," said Hapu. "It could be the ghost of the owner of this tomb."

Seth stopped to listen. Hapu grinned at Ramose.

"Don't worry, Seth. We'll protect you."

The passage turned first to the left and then to the right and then opened into a chamber stacked with burial goods. Another short passage led to the burial chamber. The room was almost filled by a white sarcophagus. There was less than a cubit of space on either side. In each of the side walls there was a recess, stacked with chests. Seth's fear of ghosts suddenly evaporated.

"That was easy," he said, examining the lid of the sarcophagus. "I think we should be able to lift this and slide it off."

He was right. The lid wasn't as thick as the pharaoh's had been. With the aid of the lever, the three of them were able to lift the sarcophagus lid and then slide it over to one side. Ramose looked inside. There was a painted coffin similar to the one in the pyramid. Ramose held his lamp up to read the inscriptions.

"It's the tomb of a princess," he said. "Daughter of the pharaoh in the pyramid."

Seth had already jumped inside the sarcophagus and was smashing the coffin with the stone hammer.

"You don't have to break it," said Ramose. "We can ease it off."

"This is quicker," said Seth.

In a few minutes he had broken open the coffin. The mummy inside was small. The gilded mask bore the face of a young girl, a child. Seth was gleefully ripping the jewelled collar from around her neck and the armbands from her arms.

The threads broke, just as they had with the pharaoh's jewellery. Seth scooped up handfuls of beads. He ripped the linen bindings from her and began roughly pulling the amulets from the mummy's body.

"Don't just stand there!" shouted Seth stuffing the treasure in a bag. "Start going through the chests and take anything valuable to the bottom of the shaft."

Ramose and Hapu did as they were told. They collected up golden bowls and goblets and alabaster vases and carried them to the shaft. Intef let down a large leather bucket on the rope and they piled the treasure into it to be hauled up. Inside one of the chests, Hapu found a casket decorated with gold and ivory. He opened it up. A sweet perfume filled the chamber.

"Look at this," he said.

Inside was a gold mirror and two silver combs. There were small jars made of jasper and greenstone, which would have once been filled with perfumes and cosmetics. Hapu closed the lid and carried it out to the shaft. Ramose saw another casket with similar decorations. He opened the lid. It was full of jewellery. There was a necklace with large solid gold beads in the shape of lions' heads. Two matching beaded anklets had seated lions threaded on them. Another necklace was strung with gold cowry shells. There was also a delicate crown decorated with rosettes of gold and turquoise. It had thin gold streamers hanging at the sides and a rearing snake's head at the front, similar to the pharaoh's only smaller. There were armbands made up of hundreds of beads. Ramose knew that if he picked up the jewellery, the rotten strings would break and the beautiful necklaces would crumble into a jumble of beads at the bottom of the box.

Ramose shut the casket lid without touching the jewellery and sat down with a sigh. He looked at the carvings on the alabaster tomb. It was sculpted with images of the young princess. He ran his fingers over the carved hair and the folds of her robes. She reminded Ramose of his sister, Hatshepsut. He wished he could do something to save the princess from the indignity of having her tomb stripped. He heard the sound of Seth grunting back down the passage.

Ramose jumped to his feet and looked around. There was a recess in the wall. It was packed full of furniture. He quickly pulled out the furniture and put the jewellery casket as far back as he could. There was some builder's rubble in the corner. He scooped it up and covered the casket. He picked up a gold painted chair and a stool just as Seth entered.

"Get a move on!" he shouted.

"I was just waiting for you to come back," said

Ramose. "There's only room for one person at a time in the passage."

"Why are you bothering with all these chairs and stools?" said Seth angrily. "They aren't worth much. I'll take out any jewels or gold inlaid in them. There should be more jewellery somewhere. Keep searching."

An hour later, Seth had stripped the tomb of everything of value. He had gouged out all the gold and jewels inlaid in the chests and furniture, leaving a pile of broken pieces of wood in the middle of the chamber. Ramose looked at the destruction sadly. At least Seth hadn't found the hidden jewellery casket, he'd been able to do that much for the princess.

They made their way back along the low-ceilinged passage. Seth was at the front. He stopped suddenly. "Look at this," he said holding up his lamp. "There's another passage."

Sure enough, hidden by a sharp turn in the passage was another opening that they hadn't noticed before.

"You go through and see if it leads anywhere," said Seth pushing Ramose into the passage.

"It's lined with smooth white limestone."

"It must lead to another tomb," said Seth excitedly. "They wouldn't have gone to that much trouble for a false tunnel."

"They might have. I'll just look at the papyrus."

"I thought you said the papyrus was only about the pyramid?" said Seth.

"It is," said Ramose hastily. "But there might be clues."

Seth's dirty hand reached out and grabbed the papyrus. He studied it in the lamplight.

"You can't read!" said Ramose. "You can stare at it as long as you like it won't make any sense to you."

Seth grabbed Ramose by the hair and shook him angrily.

"You tell me what it says or I'll—"

"Look!"

Hapu had moved down the passage holding his lamp high. The light from it reflected on something further ahead.

Seth let go of Ramose, held up his own lamp and followed Hapu. In a niche halfway along the passage was a beautiful golden statue of the god Amun with a ram's head. It was studded with jewels and shone in the lamplight.

"That must be solid gold," said Seth pushing past Hapu.

"I can't believe it's been here for hundreds of years," Hapu said gazing at the statue. "It looks like it's just been polished."

Ramose was reading the papyrus.

"Does it say anything about this tomb on there?" Hapu asked quietly.

"Yes," whispered Ramose. "It refers to several other tombs. I just didn't want the tomb robbers to find them."

Ramose read on. He had an uneasy feeling. "Don't touch the statue, Seth," he called out to the robber. It says here:

He who offends Amun will feel the breath from the lord of eternity's nostrils. The fist of Osiris will descend to end his hour."

Seth wasn't listening. His eyes were sparkling with the light reflected from the statue. "That will melt down into enough gold ingots to last a lifetime."

Seth was so entranced by the shining object that he'd forgotten that Ramose had said there was nothing about the tomb on the papyrus.

Ramose looked anxiously around the passage. He noticed a dark patch in the ceiling above them. There was a black slot about four palm-widths wide, where a hole had been cut in the smooth limestone from one side of the passage to the other. Seth dropped his bag and reached out for the statue with both hands. Hapu leaned closer to look at the beautiful patterns made with inlaid jewels.

"Don't!" yelled Ramose.

Seth grasped the statue. There was a sudden rush of air from above. Seth and Hapu stood frozen. Seth looked up. A huge slab of stone thundered from out of the slot above him. Ramose grabbed Hapu and pulled him aside. He closed his eyes as the slab crashed to the floor with a deafening thud. Seth didn't even have time to scream.

Ramose opened his eyes. Hapu was sprawled on the floor. His foot was a finger-width from where the huge stone had fallen. He opened his mouth, but nothing came out. Ramose gasped in horror.

A dismembered arm lay on the floor. Blood was trickling from it. That was all that was left of Seth.

"The fist of Osiris," whispered Ramose.

Clutched in the dead hand was the crumpled papyrus. Ramose reached over, prised open the warm fingers and took the scroll. All three lamps were lying broken on the passage floor. One wick was still burning with a spluttering light in a pool of oil.

Ramose picked up one of the lamps, which still had some of the bowl intact. He reached for Seth's bag and took out the flask of oil and filled the lamp as far as he could. He then carefully lifted the burning wick from the floor and put it in the broken lamp. Hapu was shaking uncontrollably. Ramose helped his friend up and together they made their way back to the bottom of the shaft.

"What's taking you so long down there?" said Hori as soon as he could see them.

"There's been an accident," said Ramose.

"Where's Seth?"

"He...he's dead."

The boys looked up. It was still dark outside. All they could see were two specks of light coming from Hori and Intef's lamps.

"What did you do to him?"

"We didn't do anything," said Hapu, close to tears.

"Where's the papyrus?"

"Seth had it. It's under the stone with him." Ramose folded the papyrus and stuffed it into his kilt.

"What stone?"

"It was the fist of Osiris. It crushed him."

"More like you've killed him and hidden the papyrus so you can come back later."

"We didn't! Come down and see for yourself. Seth has been crushed by a stone slab. It was a trap."

"Put the papyrus in the bucket."

"I can't, I haven't got it any more."

"Pull up the rope, Intef."

"Don't leave us down here," Hapu cried out.

"You were only useful while we had the papyrus. We would have had to get rid of you eventually anyway."

The rope was hauled up.

"No!" yelled Hapu. "Don't leave us here."

Ramose grabbed at the rope but he was too late. It disappeared up the shaft. There was a dull thud as the slab above was lowered into place.

10

UNDERGROUND

THE TWO BOYS stood looking up the dark shaft. "They'll come back for us, won't they?" asked Hapu. "They won't leave us to die here."

"Yes they will."

Hapu turned angrily to Ramose. "Why didn't you give them the papyrus?"

"It wouldn't have made any difference," said

Ramose grimly. "You heard what Hori said. They were planning to kill us anyway. He didn't want to risk us telling someone about their theft. They're tomb robbers, Hapu. There's no worse crime. Leaving a couple of apprentices to die is nothing compared to stealing gold from the body of a pharaoh." Ramose shuddered at the memory of the old pharaoh's black, leathery skin and his claw-like fingers.

Hapu slumped to the floor. "I don't want to die."

"Neither do I," replied Ramose. "Perhaps there's another way out."

"There was, but it's blocked with a slab of stone that twenty men couldn't lift."

"We'll have to look for another."

"You've still got the papyrus, did it say there was another entrance?"

"The papyrus isn't that clear."

"So what was the point of writing it if it doesn't make sense?"

"It's a puzzle. Whoever wrote it was giving directions for breaking into the pharaoh's tomb, but it's as if he knew it was wrong and he wanted to make it as difficult as possible."

"We're going to die," Hapu said, his voice was getting higher. "We're going to slowly starve to death." He turned to Ramose with a panicked look in his eyes. "And it's your fault. You should have given them the papyrus. They might have pulled us up. You could have made up a story about another tomb full of treasure."

Ramose ignored his friend's accusations.

"The papyrus mentions other tombs. There might be a connecting passage."

"Does it say there's a connecting passage?"

"No," said Ramose. "We just have to hope there is. Come on, we're wasting lamp oil sitting here feeling sorry for ourselves. Let's start searching."

Ramose picked up the broken lamp and headed down the passage towards the princess's tomb. As he walked along the passage, he examined the walls, the ceiling and the floor in the lamplight. Hapu walked behind him snivelling.

They reached the burial chamber. Ramose stepped over the pile of broken furniture that Seth had left behind and examined the walls of the recess where he had hidden the princess's jewellery casket. There were no openings. He went to the other recess and held up the lamp so that it lit the dark corners. There was nothing there either.

"That's it. We're stuck here," said Hapu leaning against the stone wall. "There's no other possible way out.

Perhaps we were meant to die in the flood," he said. "You can't avoid death if that's what the gods want."

Hapu sounded calmer, as if he had accepted his fate.

Ramose thought of all the times he'd cheated death in the last year: the attempt to poison him back at the palace, his fall from the mountain, the flash flood. He wasn't about to surrender to death now. Ramose looked at the papyrus.

When day comes, how will tomorrow be?

Life or death we do not know what awaits us.

No man can alter the lifetime that has been granted to him.

The papyrus seemed to be agreeing with Hapu. He read the words over and over again until they lost their meaning and just looked like squiggles on the scroll. He looked into the flickering flame of the oil lamp. Ramose's mind went blank. He couldn't create thoughts in his head. The two boys sat for nearly an hour in silence.

Suddenly some words that he'd read earlier popped into the blank space in Ramose's head. *The good servant stands behind her mistress.* He jumped to his feet.

"We didn't look behind the sarcophagus," he said to Hapu. "I think the tomb of the princess's servant might be behind this tomb."

Hapu looked up at Ramose without understanding. The sarcophagus looked as if it was pushed up against the back wall of the chamber, but there was actually a space of about three palm-widths behind. Ramose held the lamp up and peered behind the sarcophagus. All he could see was solid stone wall. Then he noticed a small piece of linen caught under the bottom edge of the sarcophagus. Some unfortunate tomb worker must have got his kilt caught under it as it was lowered into place four hundred years ago.

Ramose held the lamp closer to the scrap of material. It was gently rising and falling as if a soft breeze was lifting it. Ramose got down on his knees and held his hand in front of the fragment of linen. There was a faint breath of air. He squeezed in behind the sarcophagus. He felt around with the toe of his sandal. Down at floor level there was an opening no higher than a stool. There was no room to bend down. Ramose placed his back to the sarcophagus and slid down. He could just get his knees into the hole. He stretched out his feet. It was a tunnel, small but the slight movement of air told him it had to lead somewhere.

"Hapu, come on. I've found a tunnel."

Hapu got up, still in a trance. He peered behind the sarcophagus and saw Ramose disappearing feet first into the wall. He came to life and was soon squeezing in after his friend.

The tunnel was very low. The boys had to wriggle along on their backs pushing themselves along on their elbows. It wasn't easy. The tunnel was only a few cubits long though. Ramose soon found himself in another chamber. He scrambled to his feet and held up the lamp.

"There are two passages," he yelled. "One of them must lead somewhere."

Hapu wriggled out of the passage and got to his feet as well. The boys smiled at each other. Ramose could see his friend's teeth flash in the lamplight. There was still a hope. Then the lamp flickered and went out and they were plunged into darkness.

"There's more oil isn't there?" said Hapu, his voice starting to sound panicky again.

"Yes, there's oil, but we haven't got any way of making a flame."

"Where did the papyrus say this passage leads?"

"It didn't say anything. The rest of the scroll was torn off."

"What will we do?" Hapu seemed to think that Ramose could always come up with something.

"I don't know," said Ramose.

They stood in silence for a moment while the truth of their situation sunk in.

"We don't have a choice then," said Hapu. "We have to see where the passages lead."

Ramose nodded in the darkness even though he knew Hapu couldn't see him. But the truth was he was beginning to lose hope. With the darkness all around him he suddenly felt the weight of the earth and stone above him. He felt as if it was crushing him. He gasped for breath, but he could not seem to get any air into his lungs. His legs crumpled underneath him.

"Ramose, what's wrong?"

Ramose sucked in quick, short breaths, but it didn't make any difference, he still felt like he was suffocating.

"Come on, Ramose," Hapu said, trying to pull his friend to his feet. "We have to feel our way along the passages. One of them has to lead somewhere. We can't give up."

Ramose didn't say anything, but his head was filled with thoughts of death. He'd been wrong before. He hadn't cheated death, he'd just postponed it. The gods wanted him in the underworld and nothing he could do could change that. He didn't have the power to defy the gods. He felt Hapu's hand grab his and pull him along the dark passage.

The right-hand passage was high enough for them to walk upright. With his free hand Hapu felt along the walls. It was a roughly carved passage and he tripped more than once on the uneven floor. Ramose allowed himself to be pulled along in a daze. A change in the air around them told them that the passage had opened out into a larger chamber, but Hapu immediately bumped into something. He felt it with his hands.

"It's another sarcophagus," he said. "Just a rough stone one. It must be the tomb of the good servant you mentioned."

Hapu left Ramose by the sarcophagus and felt his way around the chamber.

"The tomb makers didn't waste too much time on the servant's tomb," he said. "The burial chamber's only just big enough to fit the sarcophagus. There's no space around it."

Ramose heard the sounds of Hapu feeling around the sarcophagus.

"There's nothing else here," Hapu said. "We'll have to go back and try the other passage."

He took Ramose's limp hand and led him back down the passage. The other passage was lower, forcing them to stoop.

"It has to lead somewhere," Hapu kept saying over and over, but Ramose could hear that his confidence was fading with every step.

Hapu stopped suddenly.

"There's a pile of stones," he said.

Ramose put out his hands in front of him. He felt the rough surfaces of large boulders piled on top of one another.

"The passage is blocked," said Hapu.

Ramose could hear the last of the hope drain from his voice.

Ramose reached up to the ceiling of the passage-way. The boulders were stacked right to the top and jammed in so tightly that none of them would move. Ramose sat down on the cold stone floor. He was tired. He was hungry. He was thirsty. He could hear Hapu next to him swallowing tears. Ramose was beyond tears. He closed his eyes even though it was dark. Behind his eyelids he could see little flashes of light and swirls of colour. He had forgotten what daylight was like. It was only three days since he'd been bathed in the heat and light of the sun by the river, but it seemed like a dim and distant memory.

He knew now that he would never see daylight again. It was the will of the gods. He would never see his sister, Hatshepsut glide into a room like a young goddess. He would never see the flash of Karoya's smile or hear her ringing laughter. His father would die—he may already be dead. Ramose would never be able to say goodbye. He would never take his father's place as pharaoh. He would never again see the slow, silent Nile and its rich, fertile valley.

Hapu had stopped crying. They were both waiting for death.

Ramose remembered a passage from the papyrus.

Do not give in to the terror of thick darkness.

The heart is not made strong if it is not tested.
The light that guides you may be invisible.

It was as if whoever wrote the papyrus had known what would happen to them. But Ramose couldn't help but give in to the darkness. What choice did he have? Perhaps the invisible light would lead him to the afterlife.

Ramose opened his eyes. There was no difference whether his eyes were open or closed. He'd been sleeping. He had no idea for how long. It could have been a few minutes. It could have been many hours. He wondered how long it would take him to die, if it would be painful or if he'd just go to sleep again and never wake up. He was cold. He wished he had his cloak so he could at least die warm. He sat closer to Hapu, so that they could share what little body warmth they had.

Ramose woke suddenly. He'd dreamt that something soft and warm had brushed against his leg. A noise had awoken him. A loud animal sound. He was definitely awake now, but he felt the sensation again on his chest. It took his breath away. He felt it brushing his face. He could smell something too. A fishy smell. There was another noise, a soft rumbling in his ear. Then he felt sharp teeth sink into his nose. Ramose sat up and reached out. His hands touched something warm, soft and mobile.

"Hapu," he said. His voice was hoarse. "Hapu, it's Mery."

Hapu stirred beside him.

Ramose stroked the cat from its nose to the tip of its long tail. He felt the earring in its left ear and the ceramic Horus eye amulet around its neck.

"It's not a dream, Hapu. She's real."

Ramose reached out and found his friend's hand and touched it on the cat's head. Hapu pulled his hand away as if he'd just dipped it in a pot of boiling water. He sat up. Ramose felt him tentatively reach out and touch the cat again.

"Are you sure we're not imagining her?" said Hapu croakily.

Mery miaowed.

"I'm sure," said Ramose feeling his mouth shape into a smile. "She bit me on the nose."

"How did she get here?"

"I don't know. We have to follow her."

"How can we do that in the dark?"

"She's the invisible light."

Ramose felt for the hem of his kilt. There was a small rip where he'd caught it on a sharp rock as he was lowered into the tomb. He tore it further until he had ripped a strip off the bottom of his kilt. He tied one end to the cat's collar.

"Okay, Mery," he said. "Where's Karoya?"

The cat started to clamber up the rocks blocking the passageway. Hapu held on to the end of the strip of linen. Ramose felt along the length of it.

"Where's she gone?" he said. "Has the knot come undone?"

"No," said Hapu. "I can still feel her tugging on it."

Ramose moved his fingers along the length of linen. He rested his foot on one of the lower rocks so that he could lift himself up. The strip of linen disappeared through the stone barrier.

"Up here," he shouted, his fingers feeling the rocks in the top corner of the blocked passage. "There's a hole. It's tiny. Just small enough for Mery to fit through."

"That's no good for us."

"I can fit my hand through though." Ramose reached his hand through the small hole. From behind he could loosen a few small stones. They heard the sound of them clattering to the floor on the other side. Ramose strained, his feet were slipping off the smooth surface of the boulders.

"Help me up," he said.

Hapu knelt down so that Ramose could climb on his back. He reached his arm into the hole up to his armpit. He loosened more small stones, then a larger one about the size of a pomegranate fell away.

"The passage was blocked from the other side,"

said Ramose, his breath coming in gasps. "I should be able to..." he strained and grunted. "Get out of the way!"

Ramose pushed a larger rock. It moved only slightly. Ramose pushed again, the exertion was making him feel faint. He gave the rock one final shove and it tumbled into their side of the passageway. Hapu reached up and pulled down more rocks until there was a hole big enough for them to wriggle through. They tumbled into the passage on the other side.

"I've lost the linen strip," Hapu cried out. "I don't know where Mery is."

Ramose was lying on the floor where he had landed. He felt the cat nudge his arm. "She's here!" He reached out and grabbed the linen strip. "She's leading us. Come on!"

Ramose tried to get to his feet and bumped his head on the passage ceiling. "This passage is very low," he said. "We'll have to crawl."

He felt Mery tug on the linen strip and he followed the cat on his hands and knees.

The passage continued on. Ramose's knees grew sore. Then his knees bumped into something. His hands were resting on a higher level. He felt angular shapes. He knew this meant something, but he'd been so long in the dark, he couldn't picture what it was he was feeling.

Slowly an image formed in his mind.

"Steps!" he called out to Hapu. "There are steps leading up."

He raised his head and above him he could see something bright, something glaringly white. His eyes took a while to make sense of it.

"Daylight!" he said.

It was only a chink of light, but it was dazzling. Ramose stumbled up the steps. Hapu followed him. At the top, Mery disappeared through a small hole. There was a rectangular slab covering the shaft. Ramose and Hapu pushed at the slab. It didn't move. They could hear noises on the other side. The sound of someone moving rocks off the slab. The boys pushed again. The slab lifted a little, less than a finger-width. Someone pushed a stout piece of wood through the gap. With the help from above, the boys managed to lift the slab far enough so they could clamber out.

The light was blinding. Ramose couldn't open his eyes. A hand grabbed him and pulled him along. He stumbled forward. The ground began to slope down steeply. Ramose could hear the faint trickle of water. The glare softened and his skin grew cool. He knew they were somewhere shaded from the sun. He could see an image swimming in front of his eyes: a dark circle framed with red and green, and in the middle of it a bright white curve. It was Karoya's smiling face.

11

RETURN TO
THE RIVER

KAROYA'S FACE wasn't smiling for long. "A temple guard discovered that the pyramid has been broken into," she said. "The temple workers are searching for thieves. We can't stay here."

"But we aren't tomb robbers," said Hapu.

"We're strangers with no reason to be here," said Ramose. "It would be hard to convince them."

The boys both took a deep drink of water from the waterbag that Karoya offered them. Ramose stroked Mery who purred loudly as if she was very pleased with herself. After the time of darkness, the cat's sandy stripes seemed bright and beautiful. Her green eyes were like jewels. She stepped into Karoya's lap, circled round and settled down to sleep.

"I don't want to ever hear you complaining about Mery again, Hapu," Karoya said.

"I won't. Never," said Hapu as he swallowed the last of the water.

"We have to get away from this place as soon as possible," Ramose said.

"We'll have to wait till night and then go back to the river." Karoya was anxious that they would be caught again.

"How can we travel by boat to Memphis?" asked Hapu. "We haven't got any gold."

"Yes we have," Karoya held up Ramose's bag. "I found the tomb robbers' hiding place."

Ramose opened his bag. Inside were the remaining rings of gold, his scribal tools, his cloak and his heart scarab. After Mery had emerged from the bag spitting and scratching, the robbers hadn't looked in it again.

Karoya produced bread and figs from her own bag. Ramose and Hapu ate hungrily. As his eyes slowly got used to light again, Ramose began to look around. They were in a marshy hollow where a small stream flowed. An outcrop of rock shaded them from the sun and, more importantly, kept them from being seen. Ramose couldn't believe how his luck had changed in the last couple of hours.

"We must get back to the river," he said. "I have to see my father."

They waited until the sun was setting before they started off again. Ramose watched the yellow disc sink behind the old pharaoh's pyramid, wishing it hadn't disappeared so quickly.

"Can't we sleep?" asked Hapu. "I'm so tired."

"We have to get as far away from here as we can," said Karoya. "Then you can rest."

Ramose couldn't remember anything about his journey from the river to the pyramid, but Karoya seemed to know where she was going, even in the dark. He was happy to let her lead.

After walking for an hour or so, Ramose could go no further.

"We have to rest, Karoya," he said.

Hapu groaned and slumped to the ground. Karoya found an empty grain store where they could sleep and they crawled inside. Ramose was asleep in seconds.

The next day, they decided they were far enough away from the pyramid to risk walking in daylight. They travelled through rough swampy ground and saw no one. By midday they were back on the banks of the river.

"We'll have to find a village," Ramose said. "There won't be any boats stopping here in the middle of nowhere."

They rested a while and then headed north along the river's edge. They reached a small village in the late afternoon. The villagers were finishing their work in the fields and walking back to a huddle of mud brick houses. A few simple reed boats were tied up to a wooden mooring platform. Ramose inquired about a boat, while Hapu and Karoya went in search of food.

"There's a farmer taking grain to Memphis," said Ramose when he returned to his friends. "But he isn't leaving till the day after tomorrow."

"Did he want to know who we were?"

Ramose nodded. "I told him the same story, we're apprentices sent to work in a temple in Memphis. Karoya is our slave. I said we'd argued with the captain of the naval boat we were on and been left behind to make our own way."

"Did he believe you?"

"I think so."

They sat down by the river's edge within sight of the place where the boats were moored. Karoya laid out the fish, lentils and fruit that she and Hapu had bought from a kindly woman. She gathered dry reeds and animal dung and made a small fire in the sand. She pulled the cooking pot from her bag. Ramose smiled. Through all their adventures, Karoya hadn't lost any of her things.

"The people are friendly in this village," said Karoya. "We can wait. Hapu, put some water in the pot."

"Yes, Your Highness," grumbled Hapu as he picked up the pot and took it to the water's edge. "How come you never ask Ramose to do your errands for you?"

Karoya opened her mouth to reply, when a sudden cry interrupted the argument.

"There they are!"

Ramose whipped round. The farmer he had spoken to was pointing at them. Behind him was a man dressed in the robes of a high priest.

"They're tomb robbers," shouted the farmer. An angry crowd of villagers and temple workers gathered and started to surge in their direction.

Hapu dropped the pot in the river and ran back to Ramose and Karoya. "Now what do we do?"

Ramose didn't know what to do. Karoya gathered up Mery and their food, ready to run.

"Don't run," said Hapu. "We can explain."

The villagers surrounded them and grabbed hold of Ramose.

"We're not tomb robbers," he said.

"Search his bag," said the high priest as he arrived, out of breath.

The farmer snatched Ramose's bag. He pulled out the gold rings and Ramose's ebony palette. The gold, ivory and turquoise glinted in the sunlight. The growing crowd muttered angrily.

"He is a thief!"

"That's my palette," said Ramose. "I'm a scribe."

"You're not old enough to be a scribe," said the high priest, "and what sort of apprentice scribe has a palette inlaid with gold and ivory? You must have stolen it from the tomb."

The priest pulled a linen bundle from Ramose's bag. He undid the wrappings and stared at the lapis lazuli scarab that lay in his hand.

"That's his," cried Hapu. "It belongs to him. He's not a tomb robber, he's not even an apprentice scribe, he's—"

"Shut up, Hapu," said Ramose.

The priest searched Ramose. He found the papyrus which was still tucked in the belt of his kilt. As he pulled it out, a shower of beads fell to the ground, released from a fold in his kilt where they'd been caught since the old pharaoh's collar had broken. The old woman who Karoya had bought the food from fell to her knees and picked up the beads.

"Turquoise and gold," she said turning to Karoya accusingly. Her face was no longer kindly.

"What more proof do you want?" shouted a villager. "Look at that. Beads from a royal neck."

The priest was studying the papyrus. "This could be coded instructions for how to find the pharaoh's tomb inside the pyramid."

The crowd was surging forward, ready to grab the thieves. The priest was looking at Karoya.

"What's the slave girl got in that basket?"

He grabbed hold of the basket. Karoya refused to let it out of her grasp. Others grabbed her arms and she was forced to let go. The priest opened it and Mery sprung out hissing and spitting like a demon. She sunk her claws into the priest's chest and snarled in his face. The priest leapt backwards and dropped the heart scarab. The startled cat took one look at the angry people around her and leapt into the river. The villager holding Ramose loosened his grip.

"Look!" he said, pointing downstream.

The villagers and the high priest looked down the river. So did Ramose. A huge barge was sailing majestically into view. This was not a rough village boat, it was skilfully made from cedar wood. The prow and the stern turned up and were carved into the shape of papyrus stalks in flower. The boat was travelling south, so a white linen sail was billowing from a mast. Ramose wasn't looking at the structure of the boat though. He was already very familiar with it.

"It's the royal barge," he whispered.

He was staring at the people on board. Standing

at the front of the boat with his bony, insect-like hands clasped behind him, his robes fluttering in the breeze, was Vizier Wersu. Sitting in a gilded chair eating grapes and being fanned by two of her servants was his sister, Hatshepsut. She was talking to a woman alongside her who was sipping from a golden goblet. The woman wore an elaborate wig topped by a crown. It was Queen Mutnofret. A young boy dangled a fishing line over the side. Three servants stood by watching him anxiously. It was Prince Tuthmosis, Ramose's half-brother.

As the boat glided effortlessly past, the breeze lifted a piece of reed matting that was protecting a cabin in the centre of the boat. An old man was sitting inside on a throne. Ramose gasped. The face was thinner than when he'd seen it last and the lines of age were deeper, but he knew the face well. It was his father. A young man made his way from the stern of the boat with a papyrus scroll under one arm and a palette and brush box in his other hand. He stopped next to the princess and bowed.

"Keneben!" Ramose called out the name aloud. The villagers were all falling to their knees and calling out blessings to their pharaoh. Ramose ran out into the river. "Hatshepsut! Keneben!" he called, but the breeze carried his words away and neither his sister nor his tutor heard him.

Ramose kept wading out into the river, vainly trying to reach the barge. It was as if his whole life was slipping past in front of him. He should have been on the royal barge eating grapes, drinking wine. Instead he was struggling against the river, thin and exhausted, accused of being a thief even though he had nothing but the dirty, torn kilt that he was wearing.

"Wait," he called out, wading deeper. He lost his footing and the current of the river carried him away from the barge. He tried to swim towards it, but the barge was too fast, the river too strong. His family disappeared around the next bend in the river. Tears ran down Ramose's face and mingled with the waters of the Nile.

A cry from the shore brought Ramose back to his current situation. He remembered his friends. Karoya and Hapu were still on the riverbank. Now that the barge had passed, the villagers were getting to their feet.

"Karoya, Hapu, jump in the river," he called. "We have to swim to the other side'"

"I can't swim," Karoya called out.

"Yes, you can. I'll help you."

Hapu could see the villagers turning on them again. He grabbed Karoya by the hand and dragged her into the river. Ramose swam towards them. The villagers were following. Hapu threw himself into the water, pulling Karoya with him.

He splashed around inexpertly, but managed to stay afloat. Karoya struggled and screamed and lost hold of Hapu's hand. She disappeared under the water.

Ramose swam to them and dived under the water. He could see Karoya, her eyes closed, her mouth open, struggling helplessly against the force of the water. He grabbed her under the arms and carried her to the surface. She was still trying to fight the water. She choked in air and water at the same time.

"Listen to me, Karoya," Ramose gasped. "We have to get to the other side of the river."

Karoya stared wildly at the wide expanse of water between them and the other bank. She shook her head furiously.

"Look," he said. "Mery's doing it." The cat was swimming towards them in wide-eyed terror. "I'll help you. Just relax and you'll float, trust me."

People were clambering onto one of the reed boats. Ramose started to swim to the middle of the river. He held Karoya under her arms. She started to struggle again.

"Lie on your back," Ramose said. "Imagine you're lying on a soft straw mattress."

Ramose kicked out with his feet and felt the current carry them.

"Close your eyes so that you can't see the water," he said.

Karoya closed her eyes, her body relaxed a bit. "Now kick gently."

Karoya kicked her legs. Ramose felt her body become more buoyant.

"See. You're not sinking. I have hold of you. It's safer here in the water than on the shore."

Mery swam over to Ramose and was trying to clamber up onto him. Karoya's cooking pot floated into view. Ramose lifted the cat up and put her inside the pot. Mery yowled miserably. Ramose pushed the pot in front of him with one hand while with the other he supported Karoya. He looked around for Hapu who was swimming across the river, splashing and gasping, but making progress. The river was wide. Ramose kept kicking his legs and reassuring Karoya. Eventually they reached the other side. All three crawled ashore, and collapsed on the wet sand. Mery jumped out of the pot and stalked onto the sand and shook herself indignantly.

Ramose lay on the wet sand, his breath rasping. "My father still lives," he said.

"May he have long life and happiness," gasped Hapu.

"I saw your sister," said Karoya. "She is more beautiful than ever."

"Did you see the young man on the barge?"

His friends nodded.

"That is Keneben, my tutor. It was he who

saved my life when the queen tried to poison me. He's returned from Punt."

Ramose looked across the river. Some villagers were rowing towards them in a reed boat.

"We have to keep moving," he said.

"Where will we go?" asked Hapu, struggling to his feet.

"To the desert. They won't follow us there."

There was no farming on that side of the river. Papyrus reeds grew densely on the river's edge, beyond that there were wild grasses and acacias. The friends got to their feet and hurried into the undergrowth. They ran as fast as their fading strength would allow. They kept going until it was almost dark. With no irrigation canals to carry the river water inland, the vegetation thinned out quickly and they were soon in the sparsely vegetated land on the edge of the desert.

Ramose peered back into the dimming light.

"I don't think they've followed us," he said. "Egyptians don't like venturing into the desert."

They made a camp. Ramose collected fallen dates. Karoya gathered wild grain. Hapu managed to snare an ibis. Karoya made a fire and they were able to have a small but welcome meal.

They took stock of their situation. In the rush to get away they had lost most of their things.

"All we have is the cooking pot, a few deben of copper and a cat," said Hapu miserably. "Oh, and this." He pulled something from the belt of his kilt. It was Ramose's heart scarab. "The priest dropped it when he saw the royal barge." Hapu examined the jewel. "There's a chip out of it, but I thought you might still want it."

Ramose took the lapis lazuli scarab from his friend with a grateful smile. He fingered the hieroglyphs that spelt out his name.

"At least I still know who I am," he said.

"What are you going to do now, Ramose?" asked Karoya quietly.

Ramose had been thinking about that as they'd walked. He knew what he had to do.

"I'm going to follow my father back to Thebes. To tell him that his true heir lives and that he's ready to take the throne of Egypt."

Hapu shifted uncomfortably. "I sometimes forget that you're who you are," he said.

"You seem eager to tell everybody that we meet," grumbled Ramose.

"Yes, but seeing the royal barge and your sister again made me realise you might really be pharaoh one day."

"That's my plan. I'd started to think that it was impossible. Now that I know Father is still alive and that I have friends in the palace, I know it isn't."

Karoya smiled, looking at her ragged friend. "You don't look much like a pharaoh."

"I will one day."

"Do we have to go back to Thebes?" groaned Hapu. "We've just spent three weeks and risked our lives getting away from Thebes."

"That's where I'm going," said Ramose. "You don't have to come if you don't want to."

"Of course I'll come. But how will we get there? They took your gold."

"We can walk," said Karoya.

"Walk?" Hapu looked at her as if she was suffering from sunstroke.

"It'll take a while, but we'll get there. My people thing nothing of walking such distances."

"What will we eat? Where will we sleep?"

"We'll sleep under the stars as before."

"If we keep to the edge of the desert like this, no one will bother us."

"We can go back to the river every so often to fish," said Karoya. "There are dates and wild grains. We won't go hungry."

Ramose smiled at his friends. He'd come a long way since he'd been the spoilt prince in the palace. He could walk to Thebes. He had friends to help him. He also knew that his sister and tutor were waiting for him at the palace. He felt sure he could face whatever his future held.

"The gods will provide," said Ramose.

A WORD FROM THE AUTHOR

IT MIGHT seem to us that the ancient Egyptians were a strange lot. They spent a lot of their time thinking about death. They weren't a solemn or unhappy people though. They believed that when they died they would live on in an afterlife. During their lives they prepared their own tomb, making sure it contained everything they would need in the afterlife.

Thanks to these beliefs and the fact that many of the tombs were underground, a lot have survived. Even though tombs are all about death, they provide us with a lot of knowledge about the way ancient Egyptians lived.

The ancient Egyptians lived around three thousand years ago. I find it fascinating that we know so much detail about life so long ago.

Ramose was a real person. His father, Pharaoh Tuthmosis I lived from 1504–1492 BC. Some historians believe that his 'chief' wife bore him three sons who all died before the pharaoh. A son of a lesser wife therefore became the next pharaoh. No one knows what happened to Ramose and his brothers. I thought it would be interesting to imagine the reasons for the early deaths of the princes. That is how the Ramose stories came about.

GLOSSARY

amulet

Good luck charms worn by ancient Egyptians to protect them against disease and evil. Amulets were also wrapped inside a mummy's bandages to give good luck to the dead person as they travelled through the underworld.

canopic chest

When the ancient Egyptians mummified bodies, they removed most of the insides (except for the heart). They put the insides in jars and they were in turn put in a chest. This chest, called a Canopic chest after a town called Canopus, was placed in the tomb with the coffin.

carnelian

A red stone used in jewellery.

cowry shell

An oval-shaped sea shell. The ancient Egyptians used them as good luck charms.

cubit

The cubit was the main measurement of distance in ancient Egypt. It was the average length of a man's arm from his elbow to the tips of his fingers, 52.5 cm.

deben

A unit of weight somewhere between 90 and 100 grams.

Horus eye

Horus was the hawk-god of ancient Egypt. Horus lost an eye in a battle, but the goddess Hathor restored it. His eye became a symbol of healing and is used in many paintings and sculptures.

lapis lazuli

A dark blue semi-precious stone which the Egyptians considered to be more valuable than any other stone because it was the same colour as the heavens.

niche

A space or recess cut back into a wall, usually made to store something or to display a statue or a vase.

palm-width

The average width of the palm of an Egyptian man's hand, 7.5 cm.

papyrus

A plant with tall, triangular shaped stems that grows in marshy ground. Ancient Egyptians made a kind of paper from the dried stems of this plant.

sarcophagus

A large stone container, usually rectangular, made to house a coffin.

senet

A board game played by ancient Egyptians. It involved two players each with seven pieces and was played on a rectangular board divided into thirty squares. Archaeologists have found many senet boards in tombs, but haven't been able to work out what the rules of the game were.

underworld, afterlife

The ancient Egyptians believed that the earth was a flat disc. Beneath the earth was the underworld, a dangerous place. After they died Egyptians believed they had to first pass through the underworld before they could live forever in the afterlife.

vizier

A very important person. He was the pharaoh's chief minister. He made sure that Egypt was run exactly the way the pharaoh wanted it.

The First Book in the Ramose Series

RAMOSE PRINCE IN EXILE

Spoilt and stuck-up, Prince Ramose takes his luxurious life for granted. He bullies his servants and is rude to his sister. But that all changes when to save his life he is whisked from the palace and forced to live in secret in the Valley of the Tombs. How will this pampered prince survive such a brutal place?

The Third Book in the Ramose Series

RAMOSE: STING OF THE SCORPION

For more than a year Prince Ramose has been living in disguise, travelling without rest to get back to the royal palace where he can regain his place as heir to the throne of Egypt. But his journey is not over yet and he needs the help of his friends Hapu, and the captured slave-girl Karoya, as they struggle to survive in the desert.

Return to Ancient Egypt for more exciting
adventures as Ramose continues his quest to be
restored to his rightful place – heir to the throne
of Egypt.

The Fourth Book in the Ramose Series

RAMOSE: THE WRATH OF RA